They waded on, and now the sound was nearer...

They rounded another tight bend in the underground river bed and suddenly saw the dark, living mass being swept toward them.

Jessie cried out as they came shrieking and shrilling down the black river, their eyes like hundreds of tiny hot coals.

"Rats!"

Not ten or twenty of them, but rats by the hundreds, swimming or being carried downstream like a fur blanket. They lifted their sharp noses, and the torchlight showed yellow rodent teeth, razor-edged...

◆─ **WESLEY ELLIS** ─◆

LONE STAR

AND THE GOLDEN MESA

A JOVE BOOK

LONE STAR AND THE GOLDEN MESA

A Jove Book/published by arrangement with
the author

PRINTING HISTORY
Jove edition/May 1985

ISBN: 0-515-08191-4

Jove books are published by The Berkley Publishing Group,
200 Madison Avenue, New York, N.Y. 10016. The words
"A JOVE BOOK" and the "J" with sunburst are trademarks
belonging to Jove Publications, Inc.

PRINTED IN THE UNITED STATES OF AMERICA

Chapter 1

The whistle rang out again. Across the night-darkened desert a coyote turned its head briefly and then returned to baying at the pale rising moon. White smoke spewed from the locomotive's diamond-shaped stack and ran back along the spine of the train, dissipating in curlicues and puffballs behind the red caboose.

Inside the private car just ahead of the caboose, a sleek honey-blonde woman dressed for dinner. Her name was Jessica Starbuck, and if she paused a little longer than necessary before the mirror as she slipped into her camisole, she could easily be forgiven.

A lot of men had lingered a lot longer, looking at the full high breasts, the long tapered legs and generous hips. A lot of them had felt their pulses quicken at a glance from those green eyes, at a smile.

She was totally feminine, Jessie Starbuck. All woman. She finished dressing now, putting on another petticoat and then her green velvet dress, which was a little warm for the desert country even at this time of evening, but she hadn't had a chance to wear it for a while.

1

After buttoning her shoes, she finished dressing by tucking a little ivory-handled, engraved derringer into the garter holster just above her knee.

She patted her hair once more and then turned away from the mirror as someone tapped at her compartment door.

"Yes?"

"Are you ready to eat now?" Ki opened the door and peered in. He wore a blue-gray tweed suit and a blue shirt with a black string tie. His straight dark hair had been brushed to a gloss. His dark Oriental eyes were alert and a little admiring as he smiled at Jessie.

"All ready," she answered, turning in a slow circle to show off her dress.

The railroad car belonged to the Starbuck business empire. It was equipped with four sleeping compartments, a bar, crystal chandeliers, a conference room, and a dining compartment, but it hadn't been used for a while and there was presently no kitchen staff, so Jessie and Ki had to use the railroad dining car.

They turned the lamp down and went out, walking over the deep red carpet to the door.

Sound and smoke rushed over them as they opened the compartment door and started forward. The train rocked along. Jessie could smell sage and greasewood. The door closed behind them and there was no sound, no scent but that of polished wood as they walked along the lush carpeting of the Pullman. The next car up was the diner. A dozen people sat at small round tables tended by two black waiters in white jackets.

"Miss Starbuck, Miss Starbuck," the older waiter said, smiling, lowering his silver-haired head slightly. "Such a pleasure to have you with us. Haven't seen you since your father brought you on the old Dallas Special when you were maybe seven, eight years old."

2

They were shown to a corner table. Eyes followed Jessie and Ki as they crossed the car, but then eyes always followed Jessica Starbuck.

"Who is that?" Ki asked quietly. He nodded toward a tall, dark man with a strong nose, broad forehead, and narrow lips. He was in his late twenties, arrogant-looking.

"I don't know," Jessie shrugged.

"I have seen him before. Somewhere." But Ki couldn't bring the memory to the front of his mind.

That didn't mean he forgot about the man. Too much could be lost by ignoring coincidences, little prodding messages sent by the subconscious mind. Jessie and Ki had lived too long in the path of violence to grow too comfortable.

The war had gone on for a long while. It had started before Jessie's birth, when her father was not much older than Jessie was now. While the ambitious young Alex Starbuck was sowing the seeds of the international network of businesses that bore his name, he had antagonized the leadership of a powerful European alliance of incredibly wealthy but completely unscrupulous men whose aim was nothing less than the commercial and political domination of the entire world. The war that ensued was as bloody a conflict as many another war, though its battles went largely unchronicled in the popular press and the history books, and were often fought with gold and silver rather than bullets.

But sometimes they were fought that way, too, and the deaths were as real and tragic as those that befell the victims of other wars. Ultimately, Jessie lost first her mother and then her father at the hands of the cartel's assassins.

Alex Starbuck was gone, but the cartel went on, and so did Jessie, uncovering its corruption and thwarting its attempts to bleed America of its precious resources. She was her father's daughter and she was a fighter. Ki, half-

Japanese, half-American, a martial-arts master, was equally a fighter, and his life was dedicated to Jessica Starbuck.

"Here he comes," Jessie said.

Ki glanced across the car. The tall dark man was striding toward them. Ki noticed that he maintained his balance easily, that his movements were light and swift. A rolling ship's deck or a railroad car could make a man look awkward. Not this one. Perhaps he had been a sailor.

Or perhaps he was a warrior.

"Miss Starbuck?" The tall man stood over them.

"Yes."

"I overheard the waiter addressing you. Forgive the interruption. My name is Andojar."

"Only Andojar?"

He smiled easily. "Yes, only Andojar."

Jessie's eyes measured the man, taking in the width of his shoulders, the animallike grace of movement, the strong column of copper flesh which was his throat, the competent, bronzed, but not work-hardened hands.

"Please sit down. This is my friend Ki."

"Only Ki?" Andojar asked with another quick smile.

"Only Ki," Ki answered.

The two men looked at each other in frank appraisal. Ki wondered briefly what had prompted Andojar to abandon his own real name, for surely that was not the name he was born with.

"I will be open with you," Andojar said. "I know where you are going and why. Father Carrillo is a very old friend of mine."

"Yes?" Jessie prompted. He could be open with them all he wanted. He hadn't explained yet, however, why he was there on the train, riding into Arizona.

He shrugged. "I was sent to Phoenix to try to find help, federal soldiers, an Indian agent, perhaps a United States marshal."

4

"You had no luck?"

"We are far away. The people are of little interest to anyone."

Ki looked at Jessie and shrugged. The man knew what their business was. Ki didn't trust him or believe his story entirely, but there was no point in not discussing the problem with Andojar. They knew little themselves, only that the Napai Indians who lived at a small Arizona mission were being brutalized by a gang of outlaws. There was no clear motive, no certainty who the outlaws represented.

"Father Carrillo is not young," Andojar said. He leaned back and lit a thin cigar. "He has tried very hard to continue the tradition of the mission fathers at Vera Cruz. It is a small place, very far from civilization, from everything. The Napai are new to the modern world, they are new to Father Carrillo's religion and to almost anything of the white man."

"Their home is on the Colorado River."

"Yes, that's right. Once, I believe, they lived farther south, deep in Mexico, but the conquistadores chased them from their homeland." Andojar shrugged again. That was the way of the world. There were always vigorous, hungry people ready to push aside an older or more placid nation. Andojar knew history; he knew it had always been so.

"You aren't Napai yourself," Jessie said, and Andojar answered with a one-handed gesture that could have meant anything.

"Father Carrillo is afraid that if he can't protect the Indians, they will run into the hills again and live as they have for centuries—in deep poverty, with the children and the old dying too easily, in hunger."

"And without his God?" Ki suggested.

"Yes. It would be strange if a priest did not consider that."

"Do you have any idea who these men are that are molesting the Napai?" Jessie asked.

Andojar blew a plume of smoke toward the ceiling. Before answering, he let his eyes search Jessie's.

"I do not know," he said at length. "I know *what* they are—a rabble. *Bandidos* from Chihuahua, Comancheros pushed out of Texas by the Rangers, bad Apaches. Scum, but very vicious men, men unafraid to die, expecting to die."

"When men like that fight, it is usually for profit," Ki said.

Andojar hesitated. "That is so, yes."

"So that if the Indians are poor, it can be for nothing they have that the outlaws fight."

"You are," Andojar said with a wide smile, "a logical man."

Ki didn't like that remark, but he was above taking offense at every trivial slight. "It follows, then," he said in more measured tones, "that someone is paying the outlaws to harass the Indians."

"Maybe," Jessie said. "But there are men like these everywhere, who only torment the helpless because it gives them perverted pleasure."

"Yes. It is possible. Anything is."

Neither of them believed it.

Father Carrillo's letter had been filled with accounts of atrocities, with desperate pleading. Carrillo hadn't always been a priest. Once, years ago, he had been a sailing man, a man of Cádiz who had roamed the world from Africa to the Orient. He had worked for a man named Starbuck, an ambitious and upright American who believed he had the right to make money, and that people who worked for him had the right to dignity and respect.

Carrillo had been a sea captain, but one night, rounding the Horn, he had seen his Maker and returned to Cádiz to study for the priesthood.

He knew America, he spoke English, and so he had been sent back here, to Arizona, and had gone out among the Indians, teaching them the simple things they didn't know about sanitation and agriculture. A primitive people, the Napai had slowly emerged from the hills along the Colorado River, where they had run in terror from the shining conquistadores.

They had trusted Carrillo and come to his mission to speak to his God. And then the bad ones had come. Children had been ridden down, trampled. Corn crops had been burned. Houses had been torn down around the heads of the Napai. And Father Carrillo could do nothing about it.

He remembered a man named Alex Starbuck, who had had many resources, and he remembered that Starbuck had a daughter, and so he had written his letter, begging for assistance.

And so Jessie had come. It was that simple; they needed help, and maybe Jessie and Ki could give it.

"How do you come to know Carrillo?" Ki asked.

"Long ago our mothers knew one another."

"In Spain?"

Andojar made a gesture as if it were of no importance. The man was much too evasive to suit Ki—although apparently Jessie found he suited her well. From time to time their eyes met and the messages passing between them had nothing to do with Spain or the Napai.

"What is it you do now?" Ki asked.

"Little. As little as possible."

"You have money, then."

"A little."

Ki fell silent. *It is a waste of time to speak to a liar,* he thought. *What can you learn?*

The door to the railroad car opened with a bang. A rush of soot-scented wind rolled through the dining room. The clatter of wheels, iron against iron, was loud and disturbing.

There were two of them, big men wearing heavy jackets, although the Arizona night was warm. They wore torn, dirty hats. The bigger of them had flaming red hair and a mustache that sprayed out wildly beneath a crooked nose. The other was dark and cautious, but Ki would have bet he was the more dangerous of the two by far.

The waiter rushed toward them, trying to close the door, but the big redhead slapped him aside. His eyes, bleary and pale, were fixed on Jessie's table.

On Jessie herself, or on Ki. Or on Andojar.

"If you will pardon me," Andojar said abruptly, and he rose. Ki thought he had measured his man wrongly. Andojar quickly strode away, exiting through the far door as the red-haired man's pale eyes followed. It was, Ki thought, very nearly a cowardly exit.

The two men still stood there. Jessie's green eyes narrowed as she watched them. "All right," she said, "that's enough."

"You are ready to go back to your compartment?" Ki asked.

"Yes. If you are."

"I am without appetite," Ki answered. "But perhaps . . ." He looked at the two men, at the waiter crumpled against the wall.

Jessie was truly and unexpectedly angry. Because of the waiter or Andojar, Ki didn't know. "You know what?" she said. "I'm damned tired of letting people like this do what they want while we look the other way, pretend we are blind and deaf. These men are the sort we're going to Vera Cruz to eliminate."

"And very possibly the same men," Ki pointed out. "They have the stamp of brutality on them."

"Good." Jessie rose before Ki could get to his feet and hold her chair for her. "I hope they try to bother *me*."

They didn't. The two men had moved into the dining car, the door slapping shut behind them. The waiter had gotten slowly to his knees, holding his hand to the trickle of blood on his temple.

When Jessie swept toward them with fire in her eyes, the men stepped aside. When Ki followed her they closed ranks, figuring perhaps that they had found a proper target.

The big redhead stepped in front of Ki so that he couldn't pass. "Where are you going, China boy?"

"Back to my compartment," Ki replied with restraint.

"With that blonde?"

"No," Ki answered.

"Because I'd hate to see a white woman with a China boy."

"I am not Chinese."

The redheaded man turned his head and spat. A stream of brown tobacco juice squirted from his lips and stained the wall of the dining car.

"You're yellow, aren't you?"

"I am Oriental. Half Oriental. Half American. I do not know your parents, but you are undoubtedly entirely American."

"You're funny, ain't ya? You got a big damn mouth for a China boy, you know that?"

"Perhaps." Ki sighed. It was wearying. Everywhere he went, he encountered these men. The faces were different, the names, but they were the same puffed-up, self-important bullies needing to find small prey to make themselves larger in their own eyes. "Please let me pass now."

They still couldn't let go. They wanted blood.

The big one with the red hair reached for Ki. The hand was thick, strong, with hairs like copper wire on the back of it. The hand never reached Ki's neck.

Ki brushed the hand away with a straightened right arm

and then delivered a short, quick punch to the redhead's solar plexus. The wind rushed out of the big man's lungs and he stepped back gasping, doubled up. Ki kicked him in the face and he went down in a heap, his face a bloody mask as his nose spurted blood down his shirtfront.

The dark one tried for his holstered pistol, but Ki, spinning, kicked the gun from the startled man's hand. Still spinning, Ki delivered a savage thrust to the man's windpipe, and he fell back choking and gagging, clutching at his throat.

They didn't even know that they had been lucky. Any of the blows could have killed if delivered differently. Ki looked with dismay at his coat, stained with the big man's blood. Then he stepped to the waiter, who still knelt on the floor of the dining car.

He helped the man to his feet and then left the car, the humming of surprise in his ears as the other passengers rushed toward the downed men.

The door closed behind Ki and he was left in the cleansing roar of the wind, the iron clatter of the train, unable to hear the garbled chatter of the people behind him. They would make much of what had happened—too much.

It was a simple matter. A trained fighter was a man who used his entire body as a weapon, used it in the proper manner. He didn't simply form a fist and try to club someone's head. It was a simple matter, but it amazed most people, and they made much of it.

Ki took a deep breath, smelling the sage and mingled smoke. Then he shrugged and went on his way. Jessie was waiting for him in the next car, looking worried.

"That shouldn't have happened," she said.

"No. You had the same intentions, however."

Jessie smiled brightly, her eyes gleaming. "I did. I lost my temper. Well, they know who we are now, don't they?"

"Yes. If they are cartel men."

"Do you believe in coincidences?"

"You know I do. All things are related. The universe is one," Ki said. "Long, invisible threads tie all things together."

"You think these men were from the cartel?"

"I think so, yes. Hirelings sent to test us, perhaps. Now they will know we are coming."

"Why?" Jessie stopped beneath a brass-mounted lamp, the light burnishing her hair to bright copper. "Why do they want to drive the Napai from their land? Why would the cartel have any interest at all in a small, poverty-stricken tribe of Arizona Indians? Or do they? Is it only coincidence?"

"I cannot answer your questions. I can only tell you this: if they will kill the Indians, they will kill us, given the chance. I tell you that, and I tell you this also—beware of coincidence."

They passed through into the private car and found the tall, dark-haired man lounging in one of the leather chairs. Cigar smoke rose from his nostrils.

Andojar turned his head slightly.

"Well," he said, "this is a coincidence."

Chapter 2

He rose lazily to his feet, a dark-eyed man with the grace of a cat. Ki's eyes narrowed. "What are you doing in here?"

"It's all right," Jessie said. Ki muttered and stepped aside as Andojar came to them and took Jessie's hands.

"I'm happy to run into you again so soon."

"It would have been surprising if you hadn't—since you are in our private car," she said, but there was a smile playing around her lips, a smile of interest. Ki kept his thoughts to himself.

"Would you like a drink before you retire?" Andojar asked graciously. "I was able to get into the liquor cabinet."

"No thanks, help yourself again, though," Jessie replied.

"If you do not need me?" Ki asked, rather stiffly. Jessie shook her head.

"It's all right, Ki. Thank You."

Ki bowed so that only his eyes seemed to move, and then brushed past Andojar, heading toward his sleeping compartment in the rear of the car.

"I thought he liked me," Andojar said.

"He thinks you're a scoundrel," Jessie replied.

13

"And you?"

She sank into one of the leather chairs and smiled again. "I *know* you are."

Andojar smiled brilliantly again and poured himself a glass of brandy. He held the amber liquid up to the lamplight. Then he sniffed it and nodded with pleasure.

"What else does Ki think of me?"

"He thinks you're a liar," Jessie said, crossing her legs beneath her heavy skirt.

"And you?" Andojar came to her and sat on the arm of the chair. "What do you think, Jessica Starbuck?"

His hand touched her hair lightly, and then a finger traced a line up the declivity at the back of her neck.

"I think you're a liar as well, Andojar."

He stroked the back of her neck again, and a small, delightful impulse ran from the nerves there, singing through her body to her breasts and groin. Damn the man, he would have to be this charming!

She rose and walked to the corner of the room where a leather-trimmed counter stood; it had once been a bar, where railroad men and shipping magnets and coal kings had held their top-level meetings with Alex Starbuck, where the economic fate of the nation was determined.

She leaned her back against the bar, folded her arms beneath her breasts, and watched Andojar finish his drink and stand before her, his eyes giving out messages without a hint of uncertainty in them.

"You are lovely," he said.

"You flatter me. Why are you going back to Arizona?"

"So delicate." His hand touched her copper hair again. He was standing just inches away from her. Jessie's breasts rose and fell with the quickening of her breath.

"What is your name?"

"Andojar, my dear one." He drew her head toward him.

14

"*All* of your name. Who are you?"

Her words were smothered by the nearness of his lips, and Jessie gave it up. He was a rogue and a liar, but he was irresistible as well, compelling. His arms were very strong, yet he did not try to crush her. Her breasts touched his hard-muscled chest. His lips grazed hers, running across them, going to her ears, her eyes. She felt his fingers in her hair again, felt her tresses fall free as he deftly plucked the hairpins from them.

"Which is your room?" he asked, and she turned, taking his hand, leading him toward her compartment.

They went into the soft darkness of her compartment and closed the door behind them. There was pale moonlight shining in the window and no need for the lantern.

He turned her and began unbuttoning the dress, his fingers deft and skilled. His lips found the back of her neck and worked their way down across her shoulders. The green dress slid away, and Jessie turned toward him, smiling.

"I seem to be alone in this," she said.

Andojar shrugged and slipped off his coat. Jessie undressed herself, watching him by moonlight. He pulled off his shirt to reveal a strong, dark torso. He didn't carry a lot of muscle on his chest, but there was strength there and in his shoulders, which rippled as he moved, revealing cords of muscle.

There were scars there too, many scars. A long, jagged one ran from below his right collarbone to below his navel. Ki was right; he had been a warrior.

Perhaps he still was.

Jessie was naked. Standing before the moonlit window, her body, provocative and lush, was perfectly silhouetted. Andojar moved toward her, feeling the tug of her body, the swelling of his erection as it lifted and thickened. Jessie took it in her hands and drew him gently to her.

15

"And so you can love a scoundrel?" he asked, his lips beside her ear.

"I can love a *man*. And if he is a scoundrel . . . well, that's a matter for another time. Not for now, not for the bed."

Andojar stepped nearer yet, his body pressing against hers, abdomen meeting abdomen, thigh pressing against thigh. Jessie's soft, downy bush nudged against his pelvis, and he took in a sharp breath.

"Too much. It is too much to be this near to you without being inside you."

His voice had gone whispery and raw. Jessie led him to her bed. Turning back the sheet, she slipped in and Andojar followed her, his hands roaming over her body, her firm thighs, her soft, full breasts.

Her nipples were taut now, and as he bent his lips to them, they tingled with need. She lifted a leg and rolled toward him, and Andojar felt her fingers find his shaft and guide it to the soft cleft.

"So soft, so warm," Andojar murmured. "I think I am glad to be a scoundrel."

"Be a little more of one," Jessie said. She rubbed the head of his erection against the soft flesh and then slowly let him slip inside, her fingers feeling the thickness of him, the throbbing there. When his entire length was inside her, she lay beside him, feeling her own dampness against his rod.

Slowly she began to sway against him, to lift her leg higher and throw it over his hip, to feel her body soften and become heavy, liquid, needing more of him.

Andojar kissed her and she let her tongue tease his lips. A deep sigh rose from his throat and he arched his back, driving his shaft in still deeper. He reached behind her and his strong hands kneaded her buttocks, drawing her tightly

16

to him, spreading her as he rocked and pitched against her, bringing Jessie to a rapid, quaking climax that overwhelmed her body like an ocean wave pounding against her, sucking at her. She had found her completion a second incredible time before Andojar tensed and she felt the liquid rush of his orgasm.

She lay beside him, her fingertips touching his lips, stroking his shoulder, tracing patterns across his chest. "Who are you, Andojar? Who are you?"

But there was no answer from out of the darkness.

Ki awoke suddenly. There was someone there. A shadow, a softly moving thing, a *thought*. A violent and malevolent thought had awakened him, nudging his deep, well-honed survival instincts.

Now slowly he opened an eye, and without moving so much as a finger he looked around the compartment, not seeing it. Not seeing the thing that had come there.

Suddenly he did, and it was just in time. Ki saw the moonlight on the silver blade of the knife and he kicked out, rolling aside at the same time. His foot struck a wrist and the knife flew away. Ki hit the floor of the compartment and came up in a crouch as the assailant launched himself across the room at him, dark hand raised.

Ki sidekicked and was surprised to have his kick blocked expertly. He tried a *choku-zuki*, but that blow was met by a *gedan-barai*, a downward block that dissipated the power of the blow and shunted Ki's hand aside.

A second knife had appeared in the assassin's hand and Ki was just able to duck under a blow meant to rip his throat open. He threw himself back, kicking out at the attacker's kneecap, hearing a grunt of pain as his own back met the wall.

He began a spinning attack, striking out with heel and

open hand. Two of his three blows were blocked, but a kick struck home. A rib cracked and the attacker fell back, crying out with pain.

He had time to throw the knife at Ki, who just ducked it as it imbedded itself in the wall behind his head. Then he turned and raced for the door, holding his side.

Ki was after him like a hunting wolf.

Bursting from the room, Ki saw the car door to his left close. He was in it in three strides, flinging it open. The caboose was behind the car, but the assassin hadn't gone that way. He was climbing the iron ladder attached to the rear of the private car.

Ki grabbed for the man's foot but was kicked away. He leaped up and started climbing himself.

He reached the roof and was nearly knocked off again by the wash of wind and smoke, cinders and soot that blew across him. A cinder tagged his eye painfully and Ki wiped it away, seeing his quarry ahead of him.

The man was running the length of the car, his head turned back toward Ki. Then he leaped the interval between their car and the next, hanging in space for a moment before landing roughly on the wooden top of the Pullman.

Ki was right behind him.

He ran swiftly along the roof of the private car, timed himself, and hurled his body into space, landing in a crouch on the Pullman's roof.

The would-be assassin was ahead of him still, but he was limping badly. "Stop!" Ki cried out, knowing that it would do no good. "You there, stop!"

The man turned and threw yet another knife at Ki. It whispered past Ki's ear. Naked, Ki hadn't even a throwing star to answer with. His *shuriken* were with his other weapon the Pullman's roof.

No matter—the man was his. He was faltering badly,

holding his ribs. Ki was three strides from him when the man unexpectedly went to his back and kicked out. Ki grunted with pained surprise as he took a foot in the abdomen.

Careless, very careless, Ki told himself. Moments of carelessness like that could be fatal. But not here, not now. His quarry was defeated. There was no strength in his blows, no speed, as he tried to knee Ki's groin and thrust stiffened fingers into his eyes.

The train rattled around a long bend. Distantly, the moon shone. The desert floor was flat and empty but for a faraway mesa, black and stark against the sky.

The man beneath Ki shoved a heel of his hand into Ki's face, rolled aside, and came to his knees. Ki saw three things simultaneously. Desperate eyes, glittering darkly, the trestle ahead of them like darkened matchsticks, the silver ribbon of a narrow river beneath the trestle.

The man lunged at Ki and they briefly locked in a test of strength. In desperation the assassin clawed at Ki, kicked at his groin, tried to stamp down on his instep.

All of it failed. The man's heart and strength were gone. It was like handling a child. Ki had no wish to kill him. This man had something to tell him, and so he simply held him.

Yet a desperate burst of frenzied energy rose up in the killer and he broke the grip. Ki clawed at him, his fingers grazing fabric. Then, with a cry echoing through the night, the attacker leaped from the roof of the train. Ki saw him barely miss the trestle and plunge toward the river far below, which could not have been deep enough to break his fall.

The train rolled on and Ki stood there in the wind, staring back at the diminishing trestle and the glistening thread of river.

The next morning the thin, dark man was gone.

Jessie and Ki were in the dining room when the big redhead ambled in. He saw Ki, hesitated, and then came on, his head hung low. There was considerable swelling around the man's nose, and both eyes were blackened. He sat in a corner, alone and silent.

Two hours later, they pulled into the depot at the dry, empty, sun-and-wind scoured town of Yuma, Arizona.

Jessie stepped down to stand on the platform looking around at the adobe buildings, the weathered wooden structures, the Spanish cantinas with bright lettering across the fronts, the dusty streets and dusty people.

She had changed and now wore a green divided riding skirt which had a matching jacket that Jessie was not wearing in deference to the heat, a white blouse that molded itself to her breasts as the dry wind thrust against her, low-heeled boots of cordovan leather.

Ki joined her on the platform, looking around for their luggage, and for someone from the mission. He wore denim jeans and a collarless shirt, and his black leather vest which held concealed *shuriken* in its hidden pockets.

"There is no one here?"

"I haven't seen anyone," Jessie said. She put on her flat-crowned Stetson and adjusted the thong.

"This Andojar—have you seen him?"

"Not this morning."

Ki answered indistinctly. He had spotted the porter with their luggage.

A small Mexican with a huge sombrero and a winning grin, he beamed when Jessie gave him a silver dollar, beamed again when she dazzled him with a smile.

"How far is it to Vera Cruz?" Jessie asked.

"No one wants to go to Vera Cruz."

"I do. How far is it?"

"No beautiful women," the porter said. "No—it is bad there. Many *bandidos*."

"But it is not far?" Jessie prodded.

He shrugged. "Twenty miles, along the river." He told her again. "No one wants to go to Vera Cruz. There is nothing there."

"We want to go to the mission, to visit Father Carrillo."

"Ah, *sí*, Father Carrillo. He is a good man, but very foolish. There are—"

"Many *bandidos*," Jessie finished for him; she was rapidly learning how the porter's mind worked.

"*Sí*." He peered at her as if she were a mind-reader.

Ki asked, "Was there no wagon from Vera Cruz Mission, no one come to meet us, no messenger?"

"I think not."

"Where can we hire a wagon, then?"

"There is just..." The porter's eyes grew round and astonished. He was looking past Ki toward the train, and now, with a hasty, "So sorry, I do not know," he scurried away. Ki turned slowly to see Andojar standing there.

He had a thin cigar between his white teeth, and was wearing black from head to foot, the butts of two silver-mounted Colt .44's showing beneath his coat flaps.

"Is something wrong?" he asked softly.

"There should have been someone to meet us," Jessie said. "There isn't. We'll need a wagon, I guess. Horses or mules will do. We can dump some of our luggage."

"But if you wish a wagon, I shall find you a wagon," Andojar told her.

"You can find one? You know this town?"

"I know this town well enough to find whatever it has to offer," Andojar said. "Please, you and your good friend Señor Ki must be my guests at a cantina while I find a wagon and driver."

He turned then and spoke in rapid Spanish to a wizened little man who appeared from a doorway. The old man bowed repeatedly as Andojar gestured toward the luggage.

Jessie spoke Spanish, but this was a little too rapid to follow—not so rapid that she didn't understand that Andojar, smiling, had promised to cut the old man's ears off and feed them to pigs if anyone molested that luggage.

"Please, then," Andojar said. "The heat of the midday sun is oppressive, and not good for the complexion of beautiful ladies."

Jessie took his arm and they crossed the street behind the depot while the locomotive, bound for California, sat steaming and panting beneath the sun.

The cantina was cool despite the heat outside. There was a packed earth floor, a scarred wooden bar, a serape hung on one wall, a picture of Madrid.

Eyes turned as they entered the cantina, turned and then blinked in surprise, returned to stare in disbelief.

"You attract the men's eyes, Jessie."

"Perhaps." But it was Andojar they were looking at, Andojar who produced the amazement in their eyes. He spoke to the bartender, who was obsequious and eager.

"These are my friends. Please see that they have what they want and are not bothered."

"Si, señor. Yes, certainly."

The bartender nearly knocked his forehead against his kneecaps bowing to Andojar.

"I shall see about transportation," Andojar told them as he held a chair for Jessie. "Also I shall ask if anyone was sent for you. Please, relax and enjoy the coolness."

Then he turned and walked out, lean and tall. Eyes followed him, and one man in the back of the cantina growled, slapping a bottle against his table until a friend quieted him.

"You see," Jessie said, "it's advantageous to make new friends. Andojar knows the town."

"I know you are joking, or I hope so. *Knows* it? It seems he owns it or has cowed it. What is he?"

"I wish I knew," Jessie mused. "I wish I knew, and I wish I knew if we dare trust this one, Ki. As much as I would like to trust Andojar, I just don't know what to make of him."

"And so be wary," Ki advised.

"And so I will be wary," she replied quite seriously.

Chapter 3

There was no trouble in the cantina. The bartender and then a waiter came and went with eyes averted, bringing tamales and frijoles with melted cheese, Spanish rice, and enchiladas—too much of everything, but all of it good.

Half an hour later a small, barefoot boy appeared in the doorway, blinked at the darkness, and came over to Jessie and Ki's table, hat in hands.

"Señorita, Señor. It is done. At the stable of my father, Miguel Cruz."

"Your father has rented a wagon to Andojar?" Jessie asked with a smile.

"My father has rented the wagon. Please come with me now. I will show you."

"Can we trust him?" Jessie asked Ki with a wink.

"This one, perhaps." Ki wasn't smiling when he answered. He held Jessie's chair, paid the saloonkeeper, who looked fearful of touching the money, and escorted her out, the kid going before them.

Outside, the sunlight was white, blazing across the pale sky. Yuma slept. It was siesta time, the time of day when people did not work because the sun made work impossible.

They followed the kid across an alley. White puffs of fine dust rose beneath their feet.

"Our luggage..." Jessie said. The boy interrupted.

"Already done. Already on the wagon."

The stable was half adobe, half pole-and-mud. It smelled of horse, but was clean, the animals inside well tended. Andojar stood looking at a tall black gelding as the stableman finished tacking a shoe in place. Andojar turned toward Ki and Jessie, his eyes catlike, alert. When he saw Jessie he smiled.

"Hello! The wagon is around back, in the shade of the trees. Everything is packed."

"What about the people Father Carrillo was going to send?" Ki asked. "The men from the mission—did you find out why no one met us?"

Andojar shrugged. "Who knows with Indians," he said. "Perhaps they started on their way and simply decided not to come. Maybe the fishing was good, and so they did not worry themselves about this."

"You found out nothing?" Ki persisted.

Andojar's eyes lost all their humor. "If they did not arrive, Señor Ki, how could I discover why they are not here?"

The two men's eyes locked for a moment. Jessie saw the stableman bite at his lower lip and cringe. Ki's gaze was neither hostile nor challenging, just implacable. Eventually Andojar shrugged and smiled.

"The heat of the day, you see? It makes us edgy. I am sorry if I offended you, Señor Ki."

"You did not offend me, sir," Ki answered softly. Under his breath he added, "But still I wonder. I do wonder about you."

A minute later he wondered a little more. Ki and Jessie

were taken to their waiting wagon. The cottonwoods overhead rustled in the dry breeze. The red ants were everywhere in the sand. Bareheaded, the stableman handed the reins up to Ki.

"What do we pay you?" Jessie asked.

"All taken care of—no pay." The man shook his head and actually stepped away as Ki tried to press two dollars on him.

Andojar was beside them suddenly on the black horse, which tossed its head and sent its mane swirling around its massively muscled neck.

"I must run several errands. I will catch up with you on the road to Vera Cruz. *Buenos dias!*"

And then he was gone, heeling his horse from the yard, sending clouds of sandy dust skyward. Before the dust had settled, three men with rifles appeared, looking around anxiously. Two were Spanish, one an American. All three wore badges.

"A man on a black horse just left here. Did you see which way he went?"

"No," Jessie answered.

"A tall man, wearing silver-mounted Colts. You must have seen him, lady."

"No, I'm sorry, I didn't."

"How about him?" The lawman nodded at Ki.

"My servant," Jessie answered, "doesn't speak English."

The sheriff stared at Ki for a time, and then, cursing, turned away to badger the stableman, who knew nothing at all. Ki muttered "Thanks a lot," snapped the reins to start the team forward, and headed southward out of Yuma.

After a time, when the silt-laden Colorado River appeared, low and winding, Ki turned south to follow it. He said, "May your servant speak?"

27

"Yes," Jessie answered brightly.

"Andojar is an outlaw."

"So it seems," Jessie agreed.

"That was all I wanted to say."

Jessie didn't answer. She had taken her hat off and placed it on her lap. The wind swept her hair out behind her. The cottonwood trees that crowded the riverbank here cooled them, as did the proximity of the ancient river.

Ki started to speak again, but then fell silent. They had known all along that Andojar was being far from honest with them. Now they knew that the law wanted him. What else did they know? Nothing.

They were going on instincts—Jessie's were that he was a good man beneath the veneer of threat. Maybe she was right, maybe not. Ki glanced at her, liking the soft flow of her light hair, hoping for her sake that she was right.

He came up out of the trees to join them—a man on a black horse dressed in black, his teeth flashing yet another wide and disarming smile.

Ki held the team up.

"Is there anyone behind you?" Andojar asked.

"I saw no one," Ki responded.

"Good. These men—I do not know who they are. They mistook me for someone else, I think. They would not listen to an explanation. I thought it better to leave so that there was no chance Jessie would be hurt."

"You have to admit," Jessie said, "that even his explanations are pretty."

Ki had to smile. The man was a liar; perhaps they would never know who he was. But Ki would try to find out.

Andojar tied his black horse behind the wagon and stepped up to take the reins from Ki, who complained about the lack of room and then climbed into the back to sit beside the trunks.

"A beautiful day. Such a broad and lovely land," Andojar

28

said, and that was the truth, for a change. Sunlight glittered on the shallow river and highlighted the yellow-green leaves of the cottonwoods. Distantly, a massive red mesa stood against the white-blue sky.

"It is an ancient land, as well," Andojar said. "Much has happened in this desert, much that modern man knows nothing about, will never know about."

"The conquistadores, you mean?"

"Yes. Oh yes, but there was much history made here before that time. It was only two hundred years ago that the Spanish came. Before that, for uncounted ages, the Indians alone lived here."

"The Napai."

"The Napai and the Yuma and the Cocopa, but before all of these, even older tribes who built cliff dwellings and practiced agriculture on the high mesas. People who came and scratched strange designs in their cave homes, who painted magic circles and sacred snakes and suns and unreadable symbols—and then faded away."

"The Spaniards drove them out?" Jessie asked.

"No. Before the Spaniards came, they were gone. Perhaps a savage band of roving Apaches killed them off. Some say it must have been disease. The Napai will tell you that a silver moon descended and took them all away from the Mesa Grande"—he pointed toward the wide mesa rising before them—"but that is the way of the Indian mind. If there is no explanation, the Indian will invent one."

"They are hardly alone in that," Ki said, and Andojar laughed.

"No, my friend, they are not."

They drove in silence for a time after that, following the reddish, shallow river. Birds sang in the trees, and meadowlarks lifted from the grass at their approach. The grass extended back from the river only a hundred feet or so, sometimes much less, then the land became dotted with

29

sage, until that too found the land too arid and there was nothing but sand flats, searing, cracked salt *playas,* empty desert.

"Life is difficult here," Jessie said.

"Life is difficult everywhere, but here—yes. Everything that lives must have spines and venom or a horny hide. All must live with little water, with the knowledge that Mother Colorado is all that brings life to this desert, that to travel far from her is to risk death."

"Is that it?" Jessie asked. Her pointing finger lifted southward. "Is that Vera Cruz?"

"Yes, so it seems. Good. Another hour, perhaps, and we will be there."

"Stop," Ki said. Then, when Andojar did not respond, "Stop the wagon, Andojar!"

Startled, the tall man reined in. Ki leaped from the bed of the wagon. Jessie went with him. Andojar held the team.

Ki wove through the ocotillo and cholla cactus, searching for the patch of color, the unusual shape he had seen, the form that did not belong there among the cactus. A sidewinder shuttled away. Ki watched it with narrowing eyes. He had heard it said that the sidewinder, which lay lurking in the sand, only its eyes showing, was the only snake that would deliberately attack. It did not sound likely, but Ki did not intend to find out if the rattler was so inclined.

"What is it?" Jessie was beside him, panting. She had her derringer in her hand. Ki nodded at it.

"You will not need that, Jessie."

And then she, too, saw them.

The wagon had been turned over and been broken to kindling. Beside it they lay. Two men, both middle-aged, both Indian, both wearing the white cotton clothes of peons, both wearing crosses around their necks. Both of their necks were broken.

30

Flies walked across their unmoving mahogany faces. Ki angrily chased the flies away and they lifted and buzzed angrily and swarmed before settling again as Ki closed their eyes.

"Let us go."

"Shouldn't we take them with us?" Jessie asked.

"Not in this heat. Already they have been here too long."

"And now we know what happened to our guides."

"We know that—and little else." Ki looked to the low hills across the river, to the mesa, which was now slightly to the east of them. He wiped a droplet of sweat from his eyebrow and took Jessie's arm.

"Let's go back to the wagon. We can do nothing but carry the unhappy news to Father Carrillo."

"What was it?" Andojar asked when they got back. He was leaning against the wagon wheel, smoking. Ki told him exactly what it had been.

"A shame," Andojar said. "Yes, life is very hard on the desert."

He smiled, and again Ki found he did not like the man's smile. Jessie seemed unworried by Andojar's callousness, if that was what it was. She let him take her hand and help her into the wagon box.

They started forward, moving now through head-high sage and towering "coachman's whips"—red-flowering ocotillo—and mesquite.

They went up a sandy rise and then down the other side toward the river crossing. It was there that the outlaws hit them.

There were half a dozen of them. They came out of the brush across the river, their guns ready, but apparently they had expected no trouble. They weren't prepared for what happened next.

Ki rose from the back of the wagon as the two Mexicans

to his right charged at them, sombreros flying from their drawstrings, their horses kicking up silver fans of water. In each hand was a *shuriken*.

Ki zipped the throwing star in his right hand toward the throat of the outlaw to the left, and it cut through gristle and arteries like a meat cleaver. The Mexican grabbed at his throat, finding only the very tip of the imbedded *shuriken* to tug at. It didn't matter, he was already dead.

A bullet sang past Ki and gouged a handful of splinters from the side of the wagon bed before he crouched and, left-handed, spun his deadly star toward the second man. The *shuriken* buried itself in the *bandido*'s eye. He fell from his horse to be dragged away, his boot caught in his stirrup.

Ki turned to fight off the remaining four outlaws, but there was little need for help.

Jessie had tugged her derringer from behind her belt, and as the dark-bearded, filthy bandit reached for her, she shot him in the face. The man blinked, touched the smoldering hole where his nose had been, and toppled into the river.

She missed her second shot at an Apache with a face so scarred he seemed to have no features. His horse reared up at the last moment and Jessie's bullet went harmlessly past into the river bank beyond.

That left three.

Ki didn't see it all, nor did Jessie, but both of them saw enough.

Andojar came to his feet, a silver-mounted colt in either hand, and both guns blazed away, bucking in his hands, sending .44 bullets blistering from the barrels. Jessie thought he fired six times, Ki only five, but it didn't matter. All of his shots hit home.

The two bandits to his left took bullets from the left-hand Colt. The first was blown from his horse's back, his spine shattered by a .44-40 slug. The second got it at the base of the throat. Blood spewed from the angry wound, smearing his body crimsom before he went into the river to be trampled by his own horse.

The last man was on Andojar's right. He cut loose with his Winchester repeater, firing twice as his charging horse bucked through the water. Andojar's right-hand gun coughed once and a haze of black-powder smoke rose from its muzzle.

The outlaw was gone. His horse, riderless, ran off into the river brush while Andojar, still standing, reloaded.

"Everyone all right? Jessie?"

"Yes," she said, studying him carefully now. "Yes, I'm all right."

Andojar looked at Ki, smiled, and holstered his Colts. "It is," he said, "a very difficult life in the desert. *Madre de Dios!* The savages!" He showed Jessie where the Winchester had cut a neat hole through the flap of his coat. "New last week," he said, and then he shook his head as though with great sadness. He sat down again beside Jessie, seeming to take a great interest in the derringer, which she reloaded and tucked behind her belt again.

He glanced at Ki. "We go on, Señor?"

"We cannot go back, so I suggest we do go on."

Jessie nodded. There was no way back. They had made a commitment. They had known the sort of thing that was happening out here, they had known that an attempt would be made to drive them off or kill them.

"Drive on," Jessie said lightly, and she hoped that neither man noticed the slight trembling of her hand as she gestured southward.

They crossed the river and crested the sandy rise opposite. Below them lay Vera Cruz, dry and brown, with narrow strips of green where someone was trying to start a crop of corn. The river slipped past, making another of its looping bends as it meandered across the flat desert.

An adobe church with a belltower and red tile roof stood at the heart of the little town. Clustered around the church were adobe houses and shacks, some of pole-and-palm-frond construction, just enough to keep the heat off, but not the rain or the cold, since it seldom rained and was never really cold in Vera Cruz.

Naked children played in the streets. White chickens scratched at the dusty earth. Women carried water jugs on their heads, and old men sat in the narrow patches of shade. Their faces were ancient, the faces of another time, with arched noses, long ears, broad mouths. The faces of the old were seamed by time and the weather, as if they had been snipped apart and sewn back together. Deep lines radiated from the corners of knowing eyes, eyes that had looked out onto the desert and seen many things invisible to Jessie and Ki.

There was a courtyard behind the church with a tall, arched wooden gate, and as they approached it, the gate swung open. A boy in white went running toward the church, calling *"Padre, Padre!"*

"And so," Andojar said, "we are here."

He pulled up in the shade of an ancient oak that had been there before the church and probably would be there after the church was gone. Bees hummed among the yellow flowering acacia planted against the white adobe walls. A small fountain of three tiers burbled enticingly and Jessie got down and walked to it, hat in hand, to rinse the travel dust from her face.

The boy was back, tugging a brown-robed priest by the hand. He pointed anxiously at the strangers, and the priest patted the boy's head, whispered something, and sent him scampering away.

He came toward them, a tall, erect man, over sixty and perhaps over seventy, but with an aura of strength and well-

34

being about him. His hair was thick, wavy, silver.

"Jessica Starbuck," Father Carrillo said warmly, and he took her hand, his face bright with welcome as he studied her face. "It is such a pleasure..."

Only then did he seem to notice Andojar. His face fell and then tightened. He spoke rapidly in Spanish to Andojar.

"Why are you here?"

"To help, Father."

"If you want to help, then go away. You are not wanted here."

"I think I shall stay. I am with the lady."

Father Carrillo stared at Andojar in deadly silence, then with a shrug he returned his attention to Jessie and his expression became bright again.

"I am so very happy you came. And this is your friend?"

"This is Ki, a good friend."

"I am happy to meet you, Señor Ki."

"I am happy to meet you, Father."

"And now we must see that you are fed and have a place to rest," the priest said.

Jessie touched his shoulder. "There is bad news."

"That can wait until later."

"No. It's urgent."

Father Carrillo shook his head. "Death is not urgent; life is. Life is so very short, death eternal. I know what you have to tell me. Juan and Esteban did not return with you. It is apparent what has happened. It is what happens to all of my people. One by one..." He looked toward the sky, or maybe he was looking at the belltower, which was surmounted by a cross. "Come now, please, I will show you your rooms."

Two silent Indian workers had Ki's trunk and Jessie's luggage. They walked behind the priest through an inner courtyard where flowering trees shaded a red tile walkway.

Beyond that stood a low adobe building.

"Rest, please," Father Carrillo said as they entered the building. "Maria"—he indicated a stout woman—"and her husband, Carlos, will get whatever you need. Later we will eat and talk. For now I have an evening Mass to prepare for."

The priest's eyes went to Andojar, who stood just inside the doorway to the building, watching silently, faint amusement in his eyes. The priest's right hand slowly clenched until the knuckles were white, and then he spun on his heel and walked angrily away.

Chapter 4

Evening was a beautiful, peaceful time. Jessie, who had dressed for dinner, went out into the patio to stand and watch the doves flit against the pink sunset sky. The bell-tower was golden at its pinnacle, the cross dark and somehow mysterious. In the garden the soft scent of acacia and the softer scent of jasmine mingled.

"A night for love," Andojar said, so near at hand that Jessie jumped. He laughed, his arms going around her. "Now you are afraid of me."

"You know I'm not."

"Then what is it?" His lips touched the soft lobe of her pink ear.

"I just wonder why everyone else is afraid of Andojar."

"Imagination."

"Sure. I imagine you can shoot those pistols you carry as well as any man walking."

"I practiced long as a young man," he said.

"I'll bet you did," Jessie said. "You must have practiced many things."

"I am flattered."

Ki had emerged from the building to walk Jessie to the friar's quarters. He hesitated slightly as he saw Andojar, then approached them through the dusk.

"Is it time?" Ki asked.

"Nearly," Jessie answered. Then, to Andojar, "Are you going to join us?"

"*Sí*, I have been invited. You are surprised?"

"A little," Jessie admitted. "The priest seemed not to care for you."

"No. He does not care for me. I think he despises me more than anyone."

"Then why...?"

"There is the dinner bell—did you hear it? Come along and Ki, come along with us now. We shall have a fine meal."

Ki and Jessie looked at each other, shrugged, and followed Andojar to the rectory behind the church. The priest met them at the door and welcomed them into a large but empty, mostly unfurnished apartment. There was a crucifix on the wall and, in a smaller room, a long dark table with heavy chairs.

"Sit down, please. Wine?"

Only Andojar accepted, which seemed meaningful to the priest. A hunchbacked Indian with a single eye peered into the room and left again at a nod from the priest.

"Dinner will be served momentarily. Please sit down at the table—wherever you like."

They eventually formed themselves with the priest at the head of the table, Jessie at his left, Ki on his right, and Andojar at the foot of the table, far from the friar, half hidden behind a candelabra. The little Indian reappeared with dishes filled with tamales and corn, and placed them before them.

Father Carrillo said a brief grace. Andojar drank wine during the prayer.

"Please," he said when he was finished praying, "eat all you like. There is more. It is plain food, but filling."

They discussed the architecture of the church, and the old days when Carrillo had sailed with Alex Starbuck, then got to the crux of the matter.

"What is going on here, Father Carrillo?" Jessie asked. "What is it you think we can do?"

The priest sighed. "I don't know exactly what is happening, to be honest. There is a man called Santana, and with his *bandidos,* these filthy Comancheros and Apaches, these revolutionaries from the south, these American renegades, they are terrorizing a simple people, threatening to kill them all if they do not move from their land."

"Their land? Is that here along the river?" Ki asked.

"From here to the Mesa Grande—you must have seen the big, flat mountain. Yes, all of that and much land to the south as well. The land of their people for hundreds of years."

"Not thousands?"

"No. Thousands of years ago, only the ancient ones lived here. These people, the Napai, were pushed north by the Spanish. But here they have been safe, here they have harmed no one."

"Is there gold on the land, or silver?"

"No, nothing. No one has ever found an ounce of gold here. Nor are there diamonds, emeralds, or rubies," the priest said smiling without humor, sadly. "Nor is the land fit for anything. There is only the river, and there is much river to the north and to the south. I do not know what they want."

The one-eyed Indian walked near to Andojar. As he picked up an empty glass, Jessie saw his lips move slightly, as if he had whispered something to Andojar . . . or maybe it was a trick of her mind. Andojar's expression did not change.

39

"I was unable to get help anywhere else," the priest went on, "so I turned to you, Miss Starbuck. I remembered the kindnesses of your father. Always the kindnesses, although he was a strong man, very strong. When," he asked, "will the rest of your army arrive?"

"Our army?"

"Your men. Your people." Father Carrillo waved a helpless hand. "More are surely on the way."

"No. Ki and I are all there will be."

"You!" The priest half rose. "Forgive me, but..." he sagged back into his seat. "When Starbuck had work to do, he always brought the men and equipment he needed. 'Always come prepared,' he told me once."

"We are prepared, Father," Ki answered.

"If we need help," Jessie said, "we know where to find it."

That seemed to placate the priest a bit, and he relaxed slightly in his chair. He hadn't taken a single bite of his food, Jessie noticed.

"I am surprised, that is all. It is not that I am not grateful, of course—but the lives of many people depend on me and now on you. It is not easy to be responsible for people's souls or lives."

"I know. When did this start?" Ki asked. "Why are these outlaws here? Did they come solely to drive the Indians away? Or were they here for another reason?"

"They are here because the government of Mexico will pursue them no farther, because the government of the United States cannot catch them. They live on the border to straddle the legal fence. They commit crimes on one side of the border, then rush to the other for safety. But now there are more of them, many more. This one called Santana is a butcher, worse even than the filthy bandit who started this gang."

40

"That one is dead?"

"That one lives. That one was the son of a Napai woman and a Spaniard. He knew all of this land, the hills and the river, and so he came here."

"But he isn't dead?"

"How can he be dead, when he sits at the foot of this table?" The priest's voice rose and began to quaver. He turned his eyes down, perhaps praying.

"Andojar?"

Father Carrillo lifted his head. "So he calls himself now. It is not his given name."

She looked at the tall man, who was casually, too casually, pouring himself another glass of wine.

"Andojar formed that band of outlaws?"

"Yes."

"And he has come back?" She looked at Andojar, shaking her head in wonder.

"One hears only a part of the tale," Andojar said. "Rumors are terrible things."

"But you were an outlaw leader?"

"Oh, yes!" The eyebrows lowered. "Assuredly. The old priest has a very interesting tale to tell, and yet he does not tell it."

"Silence, Andojar. You know nothing!"

"Nor do you. Shall I tell you what I know about my mother? A simple Napai Indian on whom a Spaniard forced himself. Yes, and when she was with child, the Spaniard went away."

"Andojar..."

But the dark-eyed man had no mercy. "And then my mother died, when I was a year old. I had no mother, no father. The Napai are good people, they took care of me, but I always waited for my father to come back—so that I could kill him."

He sipped at the wine, spilling a little as his hand shook. "What do you think happened? One day my father did come back. He came and asked for my mother and they showed him where she was buried. He asked for me and I spat in his face—because he had come too late, and he had come back pretending he was a holy man! My father is this priest!"

Carrillo sat with one hand before his face, his eyes closed. "I was only a sailor, an uneducated boy. I was a sinner. When I took the woman, I ran away—I was frightened. God came to me and told me to make amends, and so I studied for the priesthood, always knowing that I would come back here to care for the Napai."

"To live with your wife?" Andojar asked with a sneer.

"I will not accept that sort of remark, Andojar."

"You have accepted worse from me."

"I have tried to make amends. You will not let me. God forgives—"

"But I do not, nor does my mother." Andojar had been intense, angry. Now slowly the anger seeped out of him. "I became an outlaw so that my father would be proud of me," he said to Ki. "It was amusing that the bastard son of a priest could be a criminal."

"And you killed in the name of vengeance. And now you are back to begin again, to take your gang away from Santana and start killing again!" The priest rose. He knocked over his water goblet. "Pardon me," he said and went from the room, his robes rustling.

Andojar tried to appear impassive, but Jessie could see the expression deep in his eyes, the softer expression.

"Is that why you are here?" Ki asked. "To rejoin those *bandidos?*"

"No."

"If it is so, tell me now. We will settle what must be settled."

42

"I have said it isn't so. You saw that I killed three men today."

"Why, then? Why are you here?"

"From a liar? What difference does it make what I say?"

"Give me your word," Jessie said. "I'll believe you."

He studied her for a long, silent minute. "Yes, I believe you would," he said at last. "Very well—it is for the people. The Napai. They are my people and my mother's people. They are being hunted and killed. I cannot allow it."

"And so you were going to fight the outlaws alone?"

"I was. I am no worse than you. I know these people—on both sides."

"Even Santana?"

"Even Santana. Yes, I know that bastard all too well. I had some idea of rejoining them, of finding out what was happening, of why the Napai are being driven off. A reckless idea," he said with a slight smile, "they would kill me more quickly than a stranger. I left . . . under awkward circumstances."

"Yes." Jessie looked at Ki.

Ki's expression gave nothing away. He would have liked to believe Andojar, if only for Jessie's sake, but to believe too easily is to become vulnerable. Ki did not choose to become vulnerable.

When Andojar had gone, they spoke together alone. The fire burned low in the rectory. Now and then the one-eyed Napai had come in, but after a few sharp glances from Ki, he gave it up.

"What can we do now?"

"Talk to the Indians, see what's been happening. See if there isn't some way to help them protect themselves."

"Ki, if we encourage them to fight, more will be hurt, more might be killed."

"Yes. I know that. Maybe it's better if they run away—

but I want to know what they think."

Jessie poured herself a small glass of Father Carrillo's Madeira and stood by the fire, one hand cupping her elbow, watching the flames. "Is it the cartel doing this?"

"I don't know."

"Who is Santana?"

"I'm afraid we don't know that, either. If Andojar does, he didn't choose to tell us."

Jessie shook her head. They had come primarily to protect the Indians, but perhaps they could protect them best by simply letting them run away, be pushed from their land. "I can't think anymore tonight, Ki. Tomorrow perhaps we can learn something."

"Perhaps." He looked at her with some concern. "Keep your derringer near you when you sleep. I can feel trouble over this place like a dark and threatening cloud. It has rained. Soon there will be a terrible storm."

"Tonight you are a poet."

Ki shrugged. "I feel it," he repeated.

Jessie put down her unfinished wine. She hadn't seen Ki so concerned in a long while.

"Is it Andojar?" she asked him, but he only shook his head and after a minute started with her toward the door, where the one-eyed Indian showed them the way out—an ancient custom, Ki thought, to ensure that your guests were not pilferers.

He saw Jessie to her room, waited a time in the dark silence of the courtyard, and then went back to his room to open the trunk he had brought with him. His war chest.

Someone had been there first. His *shuriken* had been scattered about the room, his curve-bladed *tanto* knife tossed to one side. Ki lifted his head slowly from the chest. No, it was all right, there was no one in the room now. Someone had come, however, and rifled through his belongings, apparently not caring whether the act was discovered. Or perhaps whoever it was had *wanted* him to know he was being watched, appraised, examined.

All he could do was repack his chest and roll out his bedroll and lie down in the night and listen to the storm of violence that was gathering inexorably over Vera Cruz.

Morning was bright and warm, with all the promise of becoming a very hot day. Father Carrillo was in the courtyard on a stone bench when Jessie, her hair loose, hat in hand, emerged from her room.

He stood and greeted her in a manner reminiscent of old Spain, reminiscent of his son—if Andojar was his son, as he believed.

"I apologize deeply," Carrillo said. "I was unnerved, but to have left you as I did last evening is inexcusable."

"Think nothing of it, please."

"Breakfast..."

"No breakfast, please," Jessie said, tucking her copper-blonde hair into her hat. "I appreciate the offer, but we'd like to get to work."

"Work?" the priest said quizzically.

"We'd like to talk to the Napai."

"I see, but..." The priest was looking past Jessie. Now her head turned and she saw Ki striding toward them, wearing his vest and jeans. "It is very dangerous out at the reservation," he continued.

"We knew that when we came."

"Yes." The priest looked uncertain. "But you see I did not know when I invited you that a single man and a lone woman would come. I am pleased that you are here, but I have worried about it all night—I almost wish you would leave, Miss Starbuck."

"Well, we won't, so there's no point debating that,"

45

Jessie said, garnishing the firmness with a smile. "Good morning, Ki."

"Good morning. Are we going to the Indian camp?"

"Yes."

"Many live around here, near the mission, don't they?"

"Most of these did not live here until the raids began, Ki," the priest said. "The camp is in the hills, to the south, toward Mesa Grande. I still do not see what they can tell you," he said a little weakly.

Or what we can do about it, Jessie added to herself. Well, she didn't either, but they needed to find out all they could, and apparently Father Carrillo had told them all he knew that was relevant, Andojar all he was going to tell them. Maybe the Napai could explain why they were targets.

"We will need to borrow two horses..." Jessie began. She was interrupted.

"I have seen to that," Andojar said. He was still in black, but without a coat on this warm morning. He bowed deeply—mockingly?—to his father. "I have taken the liberty of borrowing two horses and gear for our expedition."

"Our expedition?"

"Of course. I have told you of my interest in this. Besides, you will need a guide."

"I beg you, Miss Starbuck," Father Carrillo said, "do not trust this *bandido.*"

"But he had told me he has changed," Jessie said.

"You would believe that? The wolf cub changed so that he does not grow into *el lobo?*"

"And who is the father of the wolf cub?" Andojar snapped.

Jessie said quietly, "There's nothing the matter with a little forgiveness."

The priest seemed a little shamed by the remark. His face underwent changes of expression—anger, sorrow, determination. "So be it," he said at last, and turned and

46

walked away toward the church.

"You don't have to bait him," Jessica said.

Andojar shrugged. "The old man needs to be reminded that he is no better than the innocents he teaches."

There was too much deeply rooted bitterness there for Jessie to deal with. She didn't intend to try. It was only on the subject of his father that Andojar was petty or angry. Otherwise he maintained his calm almost as well as Ki— and he *was* charming...

As he helped Jessie onto her horse, his hand brushed her hip and his dark eyes gleamed. He said, "The desert can be a very empty place. There are places to be alone."

"And you will show them to me."

"That, Señorita, is a promise."

They rode out then into the blinding glare of sunlight. Jessie turning once in the saddle saw the small dark figure in his brown robe standing at the church door, watching after them. She lifted a hand in farewell, but the priest did not respond.

Ahead, the desert lay flat and white and limitless.

Chapter 5

They crossed more salt *playa*—the remnant of an ancient inland sea which had evaporated over the eons, leaving only a crust of salt, cracked and broken against the desert floor.

"The oldest legends tell of a sea here in the time of man," Andojar told Jessie.

"Napai legends?"

"No. You know we have not been here that long. The legends of the ancient ones. Once, one lived among us. He was very old and had fallen from the mesa as he tried to escape a party of Napai who he thought had come to scalp him. A young warrior named Nakipa took him to his lodge and cared for him. The old man told Nakipa much, but Nakipa was sworn to secrecy. Now and then, though, certain stories were told to all of the people. One was the story of the great sea which had vanished. Nakipa still lives in the village; he is very old himself now."

The *playa* gave way to red sand dunes, weird and delicately sculpted, like red ocean breakers frozen in time. The horses' hoofs cut deeply into the red sand.

The dunes flattered gradually and they rode over red rock

country where greasewood and mesquite grew. There were willows in the bottoms of the arroyos, but these were mostly gray and dead.

"More victims of the river's whimsy," Andojar said.

"What do you mean?"

"The willows there. Farther on you will see a great stand of cottonwood trees, all dead, but useful for firewood for the Napai. The river is unconfined here, you see." His arm stretched out across the desert. "It runs no set channel year by year. It is like a serpent going this way and then that, fat and swollen when the rains come. Capricious as a child, it will slip away from you in the night and the entire village will have to be rebuilt somewhere else."

"It once fed the dry lake," Ki commented.

"Yes. The lake, the sea, which may have been a part of the Gulf of California when the land was lower. You see, this is new land, raw and changing. Everywhere you will see where there have been flash floods, where mountains have risen up and folded on themselves, where earthquakes have split the desert floor—"

A shot rang out, and a bullet whipped past Ki's head. Without hesitating, he turned his horse to the west, toward the source of the shot. He leaned low across the withers of the spotted pony he rode, and raced toward the low hills where clumps of juniper and huge stands of nopal cactus greened the rust-red of the earth.

He glanced back once, and saw that Andojar held Jessie's horse back by its bridle, something that doubtless infuriated her.

He was into the hills now, and there was no further time to worry about Jessie and Andojar. He saw the small, dark figure afoot, weaving its way through the tangle of scrub juniper and cactus.

Ki heeled the spotted horse, urging it up a steep bank,

over a cactus-stippled hump. The horse's hoofs clattered on stone, and dust flew into the sky. The sniper was below Ki, not fifty feet. He hand-flagged the horse again, urging it on, and then he leaped, hitting the would-be assassin with the speed of the horse behind his jump.

He hit hard, his shoulder crashing into the middle of the sniper's back, slamming air from lungs. They went down in a heap, the sniper out cold. Ki had drawn his knife, ready to defend himself, to rip out the throat of the assassin if necessary. But he could only sit there in the dust beside the small, unconscious Indian woman.

A long-tailed road runner looked at Ki in surprise. It carried a grasshopper in its beak. It scurried away through the brush. Somewhere not far away a rattler buzzed in the brush.

Ki touched the woman's bruised forehead with a skilled fingertip. Not crushed. She had knocked her head against a stone as she fell, however. She was young and small and dark and quite pretty. Her nose was longer than those Ki had seen on the other Indians, her eyebrows finely arched, her lips slightly full, especially the underlip. The ancient single-shot musket lay beside her, its barrel wired to the stock, which was wrapped with rawhide.

An ant, huge, red, quick, raced across the girl's arm and Ki brushed it away. A darting hawk swooped low, saw Ki, and swerved away, screeching. Ki heard Jessie calling.

"Over here," he answered without rising. "Down in the arroyo. Over here."

Then they appeared against the skyline, Andojar with a gun in his hand. The silver caught the sunlight and reflected it brilliantly. Jessie swung down from her horse to scoot and slide down the hill.

"Who is that?" she asked.

"The sniper."

51

"Why would she try to kill you?" Jessie bent low over the Indian girl. "She is all right, isn't she?"

"Yes. Just unconscious. When she awakens, she will give us the answers to our questions."

"You don't have to wait for her to awaken," Andojar said as he joined them. "I'll tell you what..."

But the girl moaned and her eyes opened, fluttering, trying to focus, and Andojar's sentence broke off. She half sat up, but fell back and rested on her elbows.

Then her eyes opened wide and she came stiffly alert. A little shriek escaped her lips and an accusing finger lifted toward Andojar.

"You!" she said in Spanish. "You pig!"

"Easy," Ki said gently. "Don't excite yourself. Do you speak English?"

Her eyes shifted to Ki, darted back to Andojar, and then she nodded. "Yes, Father Carrillo teaches us English. We live in America, he says we must know the language."

"Fine." Ki smiled at her. "What is your name. And why did you try to kill me?"

"My name is Gentle Night. I am Napai."

"My name is Ki. Why did you try to shoot me with your musket?"

"I wasn't trying to shoot you! I was trying to shoot this scum who kills my people, and if that musket was not a broken, ancient thing, I would have killed him, too."

"Why?" Jessie asked, and for the first time Gentle Night seemed to be aware of her presence. Her dark eyes searched Jessie with womanly interest, comparing, measuring.

"Because he is a filthy pig," Gentle Night said with a shrug of one shoulder.

"Is that the language the good padre taught you to use?" Andojar prodded.

"You mock the padre? The finest man who ever lived? You, who are a murderer of the Napai?"

52

"I never killed a Napai. None of my men did."

"They do now."

"I am not with them now. I am not their leader."

"Even a pig can lie!"

"I can't talk to a crazy woman. Someone tell her I am no longer a *bandido* leader."

No one could. Only Andojar knew. Ki helped the girl to her feet and brushed herself off. He handed her the empty musket and she took it without comment. Her eyes were fixed on Andojar—fiery black eyes that Ki found attractive, challenging. When she looked at Ki, some of the fire went out. Her anger was not with all men.

"Now I will go," she said.

"Won't you ride with us?" Jessie asked. "Or aren't you returning to your village?"

"I am returning to the village."

"Then come with us."

"And ride with that—with Andojar?" She got a little excited and her head began to swim again. That knock on the skull hadn't passed away so quickly.

Ki took her by the arm to give her support. He whispered in her ear as he did so, "My friend and I must talk to your people. We have no one to translate for us but Andojar. We are afraid he will not tell us the truth. Please, ride with us."

Half of that was true. More importantly, Ki didn't want an injured woman wandering around alone. Nor did he want her to go before he had gotten to know her...

"All right," she told him. Ki still held her weight, and now she seemed to realize it and stepped back. "If I do not have to speak to him."

"No, I promise you," Ki said.

"Then let us go. You have a horse?"

"I've lost it, but it can't have gone far."

"I shall ride with you," Gentle Night said decisively.

53

"Let us find the animal."

She lifted her chin a little in Andojar's direction, and he was unable to suppress a small laugh. Jessie hid a smile behind her hand.

Taking Ki's arm, she walked with him over the rise to find the spotted horse.

"A crazy girl," Andojar said.

"I take it you know her, however."

"Slightly."

Jessie said, "Enough so that she wants to kill you."

"People get strange ideas. When they get worried and frightened, they will strike out at any target, you know that."

Yes, she knew that. She also knew Andojar had been an outlaw. And probably the Indian woman knew, better than Jessie ever would, what Andojar had been.

"Ready?" It was Ki who spoke. Jessie turned to find him and Gentle Night standing, the spotted pony between them, watching.

"I think so," she answered, and then she smiled, but neither Ki nor Gentle Night smiled in return.

They started on, Mesa Grande growing large against the sky, the cluster of lean-tos and shacks at its base becoming visible as they drew nearer.

"He cannot go into the village," Gentle Night said. She pointed a finger at Andojar. "They will kill him if they see him there."

Andojar seemed ready to deny it, but he smiled and said, "She's probably right. My people wouldn't mind scalping me or skinning me alive."

"They remember it all," Gentle Night said. "They know who is the *bandido* leader, whose people do the killing."

"All right, I won't go in. I wanted to look around any-way—a few matters of interest."

"Concerning the outlaws?" Jessie asked.

"Maybe. I don't know. I have an idea or two."

"Of importance?"

"I don't know. Possibly. Anyway, I wanted to look around a little and see what I could find."

"Ki?"

"We must talk to the Napai," Ki said.

"It wouldn't hurt to learn something about the area here, either," Jessie said.

"Split your forces," Andojar said. "Let Gentle Night take Ki into the village; Jessie can ride with me."

"I don't like it," Ki objected.

"It makes sense, Ki."

"But where are you going? What is there to be learned out there on the desert?"

"I don't know, any more than we know what we can learn from the Napai. Let's just hope that something useful is going to come up."

"And you," Ki said to Andojar, "what are you holding back?"

"Now? Nothing." Andojar smiled, and Ki almost believed him.

Jessie was determined to look around the area with Andojar, so they parted company, Ki riding into the forlorn little village that had seen so much trouble. Above it loomed the huge Mesa Grande, shadowing the little valley where the Napai lived.

"Come on," Andojar said after they had watched Ki ride away.

"You know where we're going?" Jessie asked.

"Always. It is not far."

It was three miles or so into the tiny canyon where the land changed from red to dusty brown and the air grew warm and stifling. Above them yet was the mesa, dominating all, and now Jessie began to see a few trees growing along the bluffs.

"There must be water up here."

55

"There is. A little."

"What is it you are looking for?"

"Something I have seen many times but never understood. You'll see."

"Where is the outlaw camp, Andojar?" Their horses picked their way gingerly across the broken ground and they were temporarily on opposite sides of a tall upright sandstone boulder, like a great pale monument. When they came back together, Andojar answered.

"On the far side of the mesa. At least that is where I had my camp. There is another spring on that side."

And then they were there. They sat their horses, looking down at a desert pool where palms clustered. The rocks behind and above the pool were round and pale. A tiny rill wound its way downslope like a silver snake and was swallowed by the sands. Birds sang in the trees—doves and larks—and nearby desert quail called.

"Beautiful," Jessica said.

"Yes, it is. I always loved it here."

"There's no one else around," she observed.

"No, there never is. They are afraid to come here."

"Afraid! To come to where there is water, when they need water so badly. It must be a powerful fear."

"It is. I'll tell you sometime."

"Maybe you'd better tell me now," Jessie said.

"Are you afraid too?"

"No. But I want to know."

"Very well." Andojar swung down from his horse, removed his hat, and dabbed at his forehead with a bandanna. "They think the spirits of the ancient ones dwell here."

"The Indians that were here before the Napai?"

"Yes, but they are more than Indians to the Napai. They are a spirit people, secretive and very wise, very ancient. From deep in Mexico, it is said. Down in the heart of the jungle they have pyramids where no one lives. It is said the

56

ancient ones built them and then left because the priests foretold the coming of the Spaniards."

"The Napai believe this?"

"The Napai," Andojar said, *"know* this."

Jessie could only wonder again what Andojar knew beyond what he was telling her. Looking into his eyes now, she also wondered if he had lost all of his childhood fears of this place, of the ancient ones. He was thoughtful as he looked up the long, shadowed canyon toward the rocky slopes where rocks jumbled together in strange formations.

"This is where the old man fell—the one who befriended Nakipa when he was healed."

"The old man, was he an ancient one?"

"I don't know. So they say."

"Then there may be others. The ancient ones may be more than spirits."

"Who can say? They may all have died a hundred years ago but this one old man. Or there may be many, slipping down in the darkness to get their water—or perhaps they need no water. They may have another source."

Jessie was beginning to get the willies. It was warm in the canyon, very warm, but a cool chill managed to creep up her spine.

"Where could they live?"

"Perhaps on the mesa itself. It is said there are caves up there." Andojar's eyes lifted to the great, hulking mesa, ancient and time-eroded. It had been on the desert when there was no desert. Half a mile high, its caprock had protected it from erosion. The flanks of the mesa were fluted and scoured, odd crags projecting from its sides. It had seen the eons and not succumbed to them.

"Come on. Lead your horse the rest of the way," Andojar said strangely subdued.

They walked toward the pool and then past it up a small feeder canyon where nothing grew, where the air was hot and still, where a rattlesnake buzzed from some shaded nook.

The Indians had carved their history there.

The dust-colored walls of the canyon had been inscribed by primitive tools. Andojar dropped the reins of his horse and led Jessie a little farther on.

"The Napai didn't do this?"

"No. They would never come into this canyon. Here— what is this? A serpent spitting out a sun? Creation? I don't know. Look how age has treated these carvings, it is sad. See, there is still a trace of color. Pyramids..." Andojar ran his hands over the carvings. "I don't understand this design, but these are terraced pyramids, are they not?"

They seemed to be. Much of the rest of it was obscure. It was a people's history, matters of great importance to people now dead. Time had swallowed them as the serpent swallowed the globe.

"Here is a great canoe," Andojar pointed out. "See? They came on it or left on it, or sailed to the moon on it."

Jessie shook her head. "There—is that the mesa?"

It was an indistinct, much-eroded figure. Andojar shrugged. "Possibly. It is difficult to tell. Matters of such importance to them! They needed to make sure that time would remember events, people, gods—and yet they are all forgotten."

He turned. "Come. It is warm. Would you like to swim?"

"If it won't offend the ancient ones," Jessie replied.

Andojar started to laugh, but he saw that she was serious. "You are a strange woman, Jessie, to concern yourself with them. Dead, passed away, dust in history."

"No—I honor them because they lived. As we live. And I think you honor them, too, in your way, studying the rock carvings, traveling to them in your mind."

"Perhaps." He was his old self. "Let us swim. They

would be pleased, perhaps, to see us swim and laugh and live—not offended—how can life offend the dead?"

"And after we swim?" Jessie asked.

"That is life too, is it not, Jessie? And I do not think that will offend the dead, either."

He was near and strong and she sagged against him, her hands finding his crotch, cupping him as she bent her neck back and his lips met hers. She wanted him inside her, wanted to feel the heat of him, the pulsing, the release.

"Come," Jessie said. She was opening her blouse to the warm sun, to the hungry eyes of Andojar. "I want to swim with you. I want to make love."

Chapter 6

She walked from beneath the palms with her blonde hair loose and flowing. The dry wind ran across her naked body. The trees shadowed the smooth flesh of her buttocks and legs, back and breasts.

She walked to the edge of the pool and dove in, the water flowing past her coolly, and when she rose to the surface to toss her head aside, Andojar was there. She could feel the strength of him, his erection ready, swollen, pressing against her abdomen as they stood in the water, which came only to Jessie's breasts so that they floated on the water like pink-budded melons, ripe and tender. Andojar bent his lips to her breasts and Jessie held his head there, liking the way his teeth lightly struck her nipples, his lips ran over the smooth roundness.

Her legs lifted, and as he held her to him, she reached for and found his shaft, lowering herself onto it as the water swirled around them, as birds sang distantly and the sky began to change colors with the sunset.

She sank onto him slowly, taking her time, gaining him inch by delicious inch. Andojar's face was taut with sensation, his eyes lighted with need and want.

"Not going to topple over, are we?" Jessie asked.

"Who cares?"

"We might drown."

"Who cares? I would be in you, feeling your body fitted to mine."

Her inner muscles worked at his erection like rippling fingers. Andojar began to buck against her, to grip her buttocks and try to spread her wider yet as he thrust himself into her, his eyes filled with her breasts, her tawny hair, her green, green eyes, her smooth, perfect flesh.

She felt him begin to shudder down deep, felt the trembling of his thighs as his loins began to react to the timeless stimulus, the eternal need. Jessie clung to his neck, swaying against him, whispering incoherent urgings in his ear, softly moaning herself, thrilling him with the sound of her voice, her warm breath, until, with a trembling, Andojar came and he bit at her shoulder, her neck, clinging to her as if he would crush her.

Jessie began to feel her own orgasm building, a rushing liquid thing that seemed to have its source in the pool around them which flowed up her thighs and into her warm cleft, where sweet liquids leaked out to mingle with the water.

"Take me to the bank," she whispered.

Andojar was careful not to slip from her. He waded to the shore and then stepped up onto the sandstone ledge there. He lay her down as the sky went deep orange and crimson beyond the black silhouettes of the trees.

Beneath her back, the stone was rough and warm. Andojar was slick from the water, rugged, and Jessie spread her legs wide. "Again?" she asked, and she touched him with her fingers. He began to pitch against her, looking down to watch his own shaft slide into and out of her pink tenderness. He could feel her inner muscles slacken, feel her become

62

liquid and soft, and then her fingers tightened on his shoulders and he saw that her half-closed eyes were distant, far distant, lost in pleasure, and as she shuddered to a deep, demanding climax, he came again.

He lay against her in the hidden canyon and he stroked her flesh, her hair which had dried and was now spread like a soft golden fan behind her head.

"What do you think?" she asked, lightly touching his lips, his ear.

"I think I am the luckiest man alive. I think I am very happy just now to be a scoundrel. And to be with you." He kissed her again, and the night grew silent but for the night birds and the breeze chanting in the trees, chanting something which, if listened to carefully, sounded very much like a chorus of men and women, far distant, speaking of life and eternity.

Ki waited outside the old man's hut. It was nearly sundown and they had accomplished little. A long day of interviewing people who were afraid to talk to a stranger, of watching Gentle Night bully them.

"It will do no good," she had told Ki.

"Why is that?"

"They know nothing. They cannot tell you what is happening. They can't tell you if they do not know."

The elders of the tribe, three ancient men, had met with Ki, explaining in detail what was happening, the horrors of life on that desert with the wolves around them, striking and mauling. Ki had seen graves, seen the wounded, seen the dark and frightened eyes peering out at them from the shadows of the pole-and-mud huts, the lean-tos.

The people were ragged and scared and confused. They did not know why they had been chosen by misfortune. They had made preparations to fight.

"Not to flee?"

"How can we flee our own land? How can we run away from the mission where the padre teaches us the right way of living? How can we leave the land where our mothers bore us?"

They showed Ki a collection of primitive muskets, their bows and arrows.

"You see, we can fight for a time."

"When were they last here?"

"The outlaws came the last full moon."

"A week?"

"If you say so. They came and Desert Willow was killed. Fox Tooth had his arm shot off, and he nearly died. A boy five years old was ridden down by a horse. The outlaws burned our corn."

"But you drove them off."

"We did, and we will again," the old man said proudly.

Ki was shown only one thing of significance, was given only one key to the mystery. The chief waited until Ki was ready to leave before he mentioned it.

"Three men came."

"Yes?" Ki paused at the entrance to the lodge, where a blanket formed a door.

"Three men from far away."

"What do you mean, far away?"

"I don't know. Only they were not from here. They were not Indians, not white ranchers like those to the north along the river."

"What were they like? How were they dressed?" Ki asked.

"They wore dark suits. They wore dark hats, small hats. They said they wanted to buy our land."

"They offered to buy your land, and you refused."

"Yes. This is our land. They showed us much money. Very much. We refused to sell the land and they told us

64

we would be killed, all of us. They left very angry. Very angry. Behind on the blanket they left a piece of their money. This is it."

And Ki was handed a gold piece. A shiny gold piece, newly minted. It was Prussian.

"I see," he said.

"It has meaning for you?"

"It has meaning."

It was the cartel who had sent representatives here who had tried to buy the Napai land, who was trying to frighten them away.

The cartel had descended on this small tribe's land and gone to all of this effort. For what? To what end?

"Do you know now why they torment us?" the old man asked.

"No," Ki had to tell them. "I do not know why—but I promise you, we'll stop them."

The chief only nodded as Ki handed him the gold piece, placing it in his weathered, bronzed hand. This man from another land meant well, but what was he going to do to drive out the outlaws of Santana?

Gentle Night, who had translated a part of the conversation, followed Ki out the doorway. Sunset was already coloring the few frail pennants of cloud above the mesa.

"You learned something?" she asked.

"Something," Ki responded, "but not enough."

"They do not know, I have told you."

"Who might? Is there someone who might know?"

"Only the medicine chief, who befriended the ancient one and learned his secrets. Nakipa was a hunter, but now he is a medicine chief. He knows—he knows the secret ways."

Ki waited outside Nakipa's hut while Gentle Night tried to persuade him to see Ki. And where, Ki wondered, was

Jessie? He didn't like her wandering off with Andojar, not onto this desert, not with Santana's outlaws around.

Gentle Night appeared, crooking a finger.

"Come, he will see you."

Ki ducked under the low lintel and entered a smoky lodge. It was dark in there and it smelled of herbs, of sweat, of something else indefinable, animal.

In the corner of the lodge sat an old man who seemed to have only a skeleton for a body, a skeleton with dark skin loosely hanging from it. His head was thrown back, his eyes closed. He chanted slowly, his lips moving only a little as indistinguishable words puffed from his lips.

"In a moment," Gentle Night said.

Ki remained standing. He did not know the lodge etiquette of the Napai, and did not wish to offend the old man.

Abruptly the old man's eyes opened. He looked at Ki, and then grinned. "From across the big water?"

"Yes," Ki said in surprise.

"Yes, I know you came across the big water. Have you a silver helmet? I would like to see your silver helmet."

"I have none," Ki told him. The old man looked disappointed. He had a childlike face. Old age had gone on so long that he had become nearly young. White hair hung loosely down his back, reaching the blanket he sat on.

"No helmet—but you are a warrior."

"A warrior, but no conqueror," Ki said.

"I saw a helmet once, very old and rusted. The spirits said it had been silver-bright, like the sun. The helmet I saw was very rusted. I wished to see a silver one, bright like the sun."

"I'm sorry," Ki said, "that I haven't one to show you."

"It is not your fault." The old man fell silent and Ki looked at Gentle Night, wondering. Was the shaman mad, senile, drugged, or merely foolish? She just shook her head.

66

"You are a good warrior," the old Indian said finally. "You have come to fight our enemies."

"Yes," Ki replied, "that is why I have come."

"There are many. Santana." He hissed between his teeth. "A bad warrior."

"Why does Santana want to drive your people away? Have the spirits told you?"

"The spirits cannot tell me. It is not to be known. It is hidden and we are not to find it."

"The answer?"

"The thing which is the answer."

"But you know," Ki said. "You know, don't you?"

A stray beam of sunlight glinted on the old man's eye and he looked suddenly very cunning, mysterious, and compelling. "Oh, perhaps I know many things even without asking the spirits. Perhaps the ancient one told me."

"And you must tell me," Ki said, but Nakipa shook his head.

"I cannot. The spirits do not want it."

"They can't want you to be driven from your land or killed. And if you won't help me find out why this is happening, I can't do much to prevent that."

There was no answer, only a soft susurration which Ki finally realized was issuing from the old man's lips, but whether he was softly chanting or only sleeping, Ki couldn't tell. Gentle Night touched his arm and they went out into the dusk.

"He did not help you?"

"No. All I've learned is that the cartel wants your people out." Ki smiled. "And that the old man once saw a rusty helmet."

And then Ki wasn't smiling. Something had nudged a thought deep in his mind.

"What is it?" Gentle Night asked.

"Nothing."

"You are so silent."

"Yes. Silent. Thinking."

The girl shrugged. Before them and a little below them the cooking fires were lighted, spots of heat and illumination sparking against the darkness that came on with a rush in this desert country.

"You are going to leave us now?" Gentle Night asked.

"When Jessie returns, yes."

"And I will not see you again?"

Her voice was fretful, soft, and he turned to find her looking at him with wide dark eyes, eyes that caught the firelight and briefly sparkled before she turned her head away.

"I'll be back." He touched her shoulder and she looked at him again, smiling brightly.

"And I will help you talk to the people when they don't understand the English words."

"Yes. If I come back to the village to talk to the Napai."

"Where else would you go? Not to the outlaw camp to kill them all?"

"No," Ki smiled. "Not that. Not yet."

"Then where?"

Ki was looking out across the endless desert, deep purple now, silent and empty.

"I'm not sure," he said, "but somewhere out there."

"Out there! What can—"

The shots interrupted her sentence, and then drowned it out as the sounds of rifle fire, crackling in a long concatenation, flooded the night.

"Santana!" Gentle Night yelled, and Ki, looking to the south, saw the band of dark riders enter the camp, guns stabbing flame in all directions as people screamed or cursed. A few muskets fired back and then were silent as the Indians slowly reloaded their primitive weapons.

"Wait here!" Ki commanded.

"No. I will fight," Gentle Night said angrily, and she was following in Ki's tracks, carrying her own musket as he raced down the slope toward the Napai camp.

To his right as he entered the village, Ki saw answering fire, two handguns firing methodically, then the muzzle flash of another, smaller weapon, and he realized that Jessie and Andojar had returned in time to witness the attack.

Before Ki now a charging *bandido* appeared, riding a black horse. He carried a shotgun in his fists. Ki stepped to one side, drew a razor-edged *shuriken,* and flipped it with fluid ease at the onrushing outlaw.

The star-bladed weapon embedded itself in the man's throat and he tumbled from his horse in a fountain of dust. Behind Ki, running footsteps alerted him to the approach of another man. This one was a Mescalero Apache judging by his features and dress. The Apache had always preferred to fight afoot. Seeing Ki, he decided that he had yet another scalp waiting to be taken. Ki had no gun, the Apache saw. The Apache had a new Winchester, the best there was. But he didn't need it. Even without the rifle, he could kill. There was no one better than he with a knife.

Or so he thought. He was to have the chance to find out differently.

He was too close to Ki when he raised his rifle, and Ki snap-kicked it from the Apache's hands. With a snarl nearly feline, savage and primitive, the Mescalero drew his knife.

He lunged at Ki, but Ki sidestepped and stuck out his foot, tripping the Apache, who rose quickly. Ki had drawn his own knife now. The curved-bladed *tanto* rose in his hand like a living thing wavering before the eyes of the Apache, who felt no fear—an Apache warrior did not know what fear was—but apprehension for the first time in his short and violent life. This man knew what weapons were. He knew his body. He knew that they could be one and the same.

The Apache tried too quickly to get it over with. He slashed out at Ki's throat with his rawhide-handled knife. The *tanto* was quick and deadly. As Ki's left hand slapped away the blow the Indian had aimed at his throat, the right, with the *tanto* in it, struck like a deadly snake, up and then to the right, and the Mescalero's bowels fell out at his feet. The Apache screamed in agony and fell into the dust.

"Ki!" Gentle Night yelled at him, and only then did Ki turn to see the Mexican on the pinto pony, rifle raised, charging. There was no time to react, but Gentle Night had her own musket at her shoulder and now she squeezed off, the ancient weapon spewing black-powder grains in all directions, and one very deadly musket ball straight into the Mexican. It went in under his upraised left arm, and penetrated his heart.

And then it was still, suddenly so still that Ki could hear his own breathing. Gentle Night walked to him, dragging her musket by the barrel. She stood beside him and they looked at the ruined camp, at the dead. Now the mourning songs began to rise, wailing, heartbreaking songs. A child had died, a wife, a grandfather.

Several lodges were afire, and by the light of the flames Ki saw Jessie and Andojar walking toward them. Her mouth was set grimly. Andojar, hatless, still held a Colt in his left hand.

"You take a chance," Ki said. "If they see you they will try to kill you. They think you are with the others, with Santana!"

"If it must be, it must be," Andojar said heavily. "The tribe needed me; I was not here. Now I am. What was I to do—run away for my own safety's sake? No," he told Ki,

"I am here. I am with them. This must not happen again."

"We can't stop it."

"We can stop it," Andojar said. "I can stop it. I will."

"How? What do you mean?"

"I will kill Santana."

Chapter 7

Jessie and Ki had been back at the mission for hours before Andojar returned. He was slightly drunk and a little dirty.

"Where have you been?" Father Carrillo asked.

"At my mother's grave." Carrillo tensed, expecting another diatribe, more accusations, but Andojar only repeated, "At my mother's grave." Then he walked to the sideboard and took the priest's brandy down.

"My poor people," Father Carrillo said. "What can I do? They must come to the mission. I don't know how we shall feed them all, how we shall shelter them, but they must come here."

"They won't come," Andojar snapped. "They want to be free. They want to be free and live on their own property."

"Then they will die."

"No they won't. I won't allow it." The former bandit leader sat in a heavy chair, one leg slung over the arm of it. "I shall kill Santana."

"How?"

"Return to the gang."

"Perhaps you will die."

73

"Perhaps I will," Andojar said. "And perhaps that will be for the best—but Santana shall die as well."

"It will do no good for Santana to die," Ki told him. "They will simply appoint a new leader. The outlaws are being paid by an international cartel which has limitless amounts of money, limitless numbers of thugs and killers at its disposal. You may cut off a hundred arms and the thing will live. To rid the world of this Santana may be a noble cause, but it will not prevent the war the cartel is making on the Napai."

"I can try."

"Weren't you listening?" Jessie asked with some heat. "You'll get yourself killed for nothing. You won't be helping the Napai, your mother, or yourself. It won't stop the cartel, believe me."

"You know these people?" Father Carrillo asked. "This mysterious cartel?"

"Too well. They are the ones who killed my mother and father."

"How can you be sure?"

Ki answered. "Today I was shown a coin of Prussian mint. It was brand-new. Made this year. Struck in Prussia, where the cartel is headquartered. The Napai had it. The men who are trying to push them from their land left it behind."

"This is confusing. What does it mean?"

"It means there is something valuable, immensely valuable on that land, Father," Jessie told the priest.

"But there . . . there is nothing."

"Yes there is. What, I don't know exactly—but Ki and I have discussed it and we have an idea."

"How could you know?"

"Certain small hints. Threads. When they were put together they seemed to weave a fabric of an incredible but logical pattern."

"I do not understand." The priest watched his bastard son pour out another four ounces of brandy. "Some men came here once, over a year ago. They asked to look at the old records."

"The records?"

"Yes. The Church, as you know, is the keeper of records for all of the community in Catholic lands."

"Because," Andojar said bitterly, "no one else has been allowed to learn to read or write."

"Who teaches the Indians now, Andojar?" the priest shot back.

"Please," Ki implored. "The visitors?"

The priest shrugged and looked briefly toward the ceiling. "Two men dressed in dark suits. They asked to see the Vasquez papers."

"What are they, Father?"

"Very old manuscripts. Two of them. Vasquez was a mutineer against the Empire of Spain. A ship's captain who tried to sail away with much gold in the hold of his galleon."

"What happened to him?"

"No one knows for sure. Apparently, like many other sailing men of his century, Vasquez thought the peninsula of Baja California was an island and that he could elude the king's ships by sailing around it. Of course, he just sailed into the Gulf of California and then would have been able to sail no more."

"Is that what happened?"

"Apparently," Carrillo said. "Nothing was ever seen again of Vasquez or his crew. If they tried to cross the desert with their gold, heat and the Indians would have killed them. The Napai were once very fierce."

"It's more likely the ship was sunk, isn't it?"

"Yes. But there are no accurate records. The Vasquez documents were brought to me by an Indian. Where he found them, I do not know. One roll of parchment is a partial ship's log, the other is supposedly a map to where the treasure is . . . or was."

"There is a map to that gold?" Ki asked.

"A purported map. When it was written, the idea was to conceal the true directions, apparently. It is in a sort of code, the points of the compass altered. If I could tell you how many visitors to Vera Cruz have asked to see the Vasquez papers! But no one has ever discovered the meaning of the map—and I have had historians, Spanish scholars, men who specialize in puzzles and codes throw up their hands in disgust."

"But they keep coming."

"Oh yes. That is why it was not unusual when the men in the dark suits came. I didn't feel it was important enough to mention. Do you think it is somehow related, that the Indians' troubles have something to do with the Vasquez treasure?"

"It seems so."

"But if the ship was sunk in the Gulf, then the treasure— if there is one—must be a hundred miles from here."

"Someone doesn't think so," Ki said. *"I* don't think so."

"You! What do you know of this?"

"Very little," Ki admitted. "But I do know that a rusted Spanish helmet has been seen near here."

"Then they did try walking across the desert."

"Possibly. Other exploration parties have undoubtedly passed this way, as well. The helmet is not positive proof."

"May we see the Vasquez papers, Father?" Jessie asked.

"Certainly. I'll bring them from the archives."

He rose and went out, his robes whispering. Andojar sat scowling. "None of this is helping much."

"It is as much help as sitting and hating," Ki pointed out. The man in black shook his head.

"There will be no peace for the Napai until their enemies

are driven out by force. No amount of treasure hunting—"

"Gone!" Ki's head turned. Jessie was already on her feet. Father Carrillo stood before them, his expression empty. He had two rolls of very old parchment in his hands. From one dangled a red ribbon.

"What is gone?"

"The Vasquez papers. These are blank parchments— exactly the same as the others, of the same age—but there is nothing written on them."

Ki and Jessie looked at each other. The cartel's representatives had come well prepared. They had the map and they wanted no one else to follow them. It was becoming a certainty that the Vasquez treasure was what had drawn trouble to Vera Cruz.

Father Carrillo was dismayed, not over the loss of the map, but simply because documents entrusted to him and his church had been pilfered.

"I have always let everyone examine my papers. These men returned them to me ... or so I thought."

"Can you describe them, Father?" Jessie asked.

"Not really. All I recall clearly is that they spoke with a foreign accent."

"All right. Then, Ki, do we begin in the morning?"

"Begin what?" Andojar asked.

"Begin looking for the treasure."

"But you have no idea where it is." Andojar spread his hands. "How could you? The map is gone."

"That map. The other cannot be destroyed."

"Jessie, you are a remarkable woman," Andojar said, "but I don't know what you are talking about. Riddles, riddles."

"I'm sorry. I didn't mean to make it into a mystery."

Father Carrillo asked, "Do you mean that you and Ki know where the gold is? Without the Vasquez papers?"

"We know where it *should* be. Whether it is gone, taken away by the Spaniards or by later treasure hunters, we don't know."

"Is it on the Indian land?"

"Yes."

"But where?"

"Inside a mountain. Buried inside Mesa Grande," Jessie told them. The priest and his son just looked at her, then at Ki, wanting to laugh, to disbelieve, but Jessie's expression was not one of someone playing a joke.

"You are mad," Andojar said at length.

"Possibly. More probably simply mistaken, but I don't think that's so, either," Jessie said. She sat again, tossing her hair over her shoulder.

"How could you have reached this conclusion—and if it is so, what good could it do anyone? The theory is bizarre, but if it were accurate, how could anyone ever recover gold from the heart of a mountain?"

"I can only tell you what I think," Jessie said. She glanced at Ki, who nodded, indicating that she should tell the story they had pieced together. "It begins with the Colorado River and a sailing ship that had nowhere to go. Vasquez stole the king's gold and sailed away—right up the Gulf of California. In those days, as you've pointed out, California was thought to be an island. Vasquez was a mutineer and a thief, running for his life. Suddenly he ran out of sea."

"Yes. He could go no farther after reaching the coast."

"Couldn't he? I think he could. I think that if it was a wet year he could have kept on coming—sailing right up the Colorado River."

"Where? Where would he go? Why would he do such a thing?"

"Why wouldn't he? There was nowhere else to go, remember. He couldn't sail back down the Gulf. If the Colorado was running high, he could have come up it, possibly looking for an island sea or a way back to the Pacific. He was still thinking that California was an island, remember."

"I have seen an old map that showed our dry lake to be sea," Father Carrillo said. "The Indians recall a time when it was wet. Perhaps..."

"Perhaps Vasquez had one of those maps. The old cartographers were great ones for drawing maps of places they'd never seen, sometimes of places they'd only imagined. Anyway," Jessie went on, "he had no choice. He sailed up the Colorado."

"The great canoe in the stone carvings!" Andojar said, coming to his feet.

"I think so. It resembles a Spanish galleon just a little too much for it to be coincidental."

"But," Carrillo said, perplexed, "you say he sailed up the river. Now you say the treasure is in the mesa. That makes no sense."

"The river, Father, is a wandering thing. It goes here and then there. The old riverbottom is evident. It ran right through the mesa. If you go there now you can still find signs of an underground river. A spring on the south side, another on the north. A boulder-strewn watercourse running in a direction contrary to that a flash flood off the mesa itself would take."

"But I do not see..." The priest shook his head.

"The mesa," Ki pointed out, "is honeycombed with caves."

"There are caves, yes, but I have never seen anything large enough for a ship!"

"Time changes all things, Father. I think that galleon is there. I think it sailed up a wild and whimsical river which changed its course, which dwindled as the rains ceased. I think Vasquez saw a mammoth cavern open up before him, and he sailed his galleon in there to hide it from searching eyes."

"Then he could not sail out again."

"I think he could have—at first—but time went by and the river went down. And then disaster struck. The mesa, eroded by the river and time itself, collapsed and shut off the exit to the cavern."

"You believe the galleon is buried inside Mesa Grande."

"We do. And so," Jessie added, "does the cartel."

"How could the gold ever be recovered? If that much earth has fallen on it..."

"I don't know. The cartel has money, time. They just need privacy. They need to get the Indians off the land, away from the mesa."

"It is incredible."

"Yes it is. I think that's what sent so many of your scholars and treasure hunters off scratching their heads. Even coming to the proper conclusion, they couldn't accept the truth of it. I wish we had the maps to go over, but I don't think it's necessary. The gold is there; I know it."

"You speak of the gold, Jessie," Andojar said. "What of the Napai? They are of the primary importance."

"*Now!*" Father Carrillo said excitedly. "You say that now! Before, you did not care for them. Before you turned your back on them. You denied they were your people."

Andojar started to get angry himself. He managed to hold it in, however. "A man *can* change. It is possible, is it not, for a bad man to have a change of heart?"

Father and son studied each other silently before Carrillo nodded and turned slightly away.

"If we remove the gold, the *bandidos* will go," Ki reminded Andojar. "We haven't got the forces to take them on. No matter how many we kill, the cartel will hire more. More killers, more gunmen. There will be more fighting involving the Napai. If we remove the gold, we finish it."

"That's what you two plan to do?"

Jessie shook her head. "Yes."

Andojar shrugged. "Then I am with you."

"There are many *bandidos*," Father Carrillo said. "Many guns. There are only the three of you."

"Yes. That's the way it must be," Ki said.

"I would make it four. I am coming."

"No," Andojar said emphatically.

"The village needs a priest, Father."

"The village needs to be safe from these bad men. If I can help bring that about, I will have been of more use."

"No," Andojar said again. "We do not need you. There is nothing you can do. You are a priest, not a fighter."

"I have not always been a man of the cloth," Carrillo reminded him. "I have fought. For these people I would fight again. I would pray for their souls, these *bandidos*, but God help me, I would kill them. I have not yet heard Ki and Jessie tell me I cannot go. Is it to be that way?"

Ki spoke for both of them. "If you must come, if your conscience allows it, come. If you cannot fight, if you cannot kill, then do not come."

"At sunrise?" Father Carrillo asked.

"Yes, at sunrise."

Chapter 8

She was waiting for Ki outside his room. Dawn was a burst of pale color in the east. It was warm already. Doves cooed in the garden.

"What is it?" Ki asked Gentle Night. "Is there trouble?"

"No." She sat against the shaded adobe wall, her hands linked together around her knees. "I have come to help."

"Today we will not need your help."

"You are not coming to the village?" She looked crestfallen.

"No."

"Then I will stay here with you. I can tell you much," she said.

"I am traveling with my friends."

"The woman with the pale hair."

"Yes."

"Do you love her?" Gentle Night got to her feet and her eyes searched Ki's. "Do you love this pale-haired woman?"

"She is not my woman," Ki said at last.

Gentle Night relaxed. She smiled, revealing even white teeth. "I will travel with you."

"It will be dangerous. There are still many *bandidos* around."

"I have my musket."

"Please—I don't know how long we will be gone."

Gentle Night said, "No one will miss me." When Ki started away, she went with him.

"It is very dangerous," Ki said, stopping, taking her by the shoulders, trying by his manner to impress upon her the seriousness of things. "They'll kill us instantly if we give them the chance."

"And what do you believe they will do to us if they return to our village? I have lived with war, I have lived with bloodshed, Ki. I know what danger is. I would rather be with you."

"You cannot be with me."

"If you do not take me, I shall follow you."

"Gentle Night . . . it is impossible."

"No. You just do not want it. Take me. I know the people and the land as you cannot."

There was some logic to that, but Ki wasn't inclined to give in. They had already agreed to take the priest. True, Carrillo had sailed the seven seas, but that was long ago. Andojar was a gunman. Jessie could always be trusted in tight situations, but he didn't want to be responsible for the Indian woman.

"I am not a coward."

"I know that. I've seen you fight."

"I am not discussing this any longer. I am going. Beat me, I shall follow. Chase me away, I shall return."

"But why, woman! Why do you wish to go?"

"Why?" Her eyes went soft. "I thought you were a man who saw many things," she said. "I wish to go just because it is where you will be."

There was no answer to that, so it was a good thing that

Jessie made her appearance then, a pair of saddlebags slung over her shoulder, her Colt belted around her waist. A beautiful gun that was, too.

Alex Starbuck had given it to Jessie on her eighteenth birthday. Custom-built by the Colt factory in Connecticut at Starbuck's request, it was a double-action .38-caliber revolver mounted on a .44 frame for reduced recoil. The finish was slate gray, the handgrips polished peachwood. Jessie knew how to handle it. Even Ki, who generally disapproved of firearms, admired her ability with it—and he was happy to see that she was wearing it this day. It would perhaps be a day for guns.

Father Carrillo was wearing jeans and a flannel shirt when they met him at the stable. Ki and Jessie had the same mounts as the day before. Andojar's black horse stood saddled, bedroll and saddlebags on, but he wasn't there. When he did show up, he apologized.

"I found only one other rifle in town," he said, showing them the fairly new Henry repeater. He gave it to Ki, who shook his head.

Andojar was puzzled. "Don't know how to use one?"

"I manage most of the time without one."

"You won't on this trip."

"Give it to the girl."

Andojar looked at the rifle, then at Gentle Night, and shrugged. He handed it over, adding a green box of .44-40 cartridges. "You didn't want a weapon, did you, *Father?*"

"I have my own," Carrillo answered, ignoring the dig. He showed them an extraordinary and very deadly weapon. "It has four barrels, as you see. An eight-gauge shotgun made in Germany."

The bores looked big enough to shove a fist down, and it looked heavy. The barrels, all four of them, were two and a half feet long, built around a center rod. Fine whorls of Damascus steel showed on the barrels. Engraving ran over the trigger guard and butt plate.

"Father, what have you got a thing like that for?" Andojar said. He took it once and hefted it. It was as heavy as it looked.

"A man walks many paths in this life," the priest said. He took the weapon back and slung it over his shoulder on its broad leather strap.

They filled their canteens and water sacks then, and let the horses have a last drink before they started out beneath the pale desert sky toward the hulking mesa beyond.

Jessie and Ki rode side by side, both silent for a while, both thoughtful. Finally Ki broke the silence.

"There must be a way in, Jessie. They can't be planning on blowing the mesa up, and it would take a team of engineers a lifetime to excavate. There must be a way!"

"Maybe. Maybe there is no way at all, and they haven't yet discovered that unhappy fact."

"I don't believe that. There is the map, for one thing— it survived. It must have been brought up from the mesa cavern."

"Maybe. What do the Indians say? Is there a way in? A tunnel? A sign of a cave?"

"Not that I have heard. But there must be. There *must* be."

Or did there have to be? If there was an easy way, then someone would have used it already, someone would already have recovered the treasure. He talked to Gentle Night about it.

"Is there a way? Andojar says there are caves there, but is there a deep cave, a tunnel, anything that might lead to the heart of the mountain?"

"No!" She answered sharply.

"Why do you answer me like that?"

"I don't know."

"It is a simple question. If you don't care to answer it, say so."

"I don't know."

"What is worrying you?"

"I didn't know we were going to Mesa Grande."

"And if we are?"

"Nothing."

"You can turn back," he told her.

"No. I will go on."

"You haven't answered my question." The horses plodded on side by side across the pale earth. A crow sailed against the white sky, cawing. The mesa grew larger, and Gentle Night looked to it now, her eyes revealing fear.

"I don't know."

"But you have heard something. Perhaps from Nakipa. Did he tell you something?"

"I don't know!"

"What is it?" Ki asked. "What are you afraid of?"

"It is a spirit place!" she nearly shouted. "No one can go to the mesa. The ancient ones do not like it."

"The ancient ones are all dead."

"The ancient ones live!"

"As spirits."

"No one can go to the mesa," she said again. "It is not right. Bad things are there."

"Then return home."

"No. I won't leave you to the bad spirits."

Ki tried to reassure her. "We have the priest with us. How can the spirits bother us?"

Gentle Night turned that over in her mind for a while, and seemed to relax slightly. "He doesn't have his robes on. How will the spirits know he is a priest?"

"They will know."

She still looked doubtful. "They are not all dead," was what she said.

Ki pulled back on the reins, halted his horse, and sat there in the heat and swirling sand, staring at her.

"What did you say?"

"They are not all dead. There are more ancient ones. They live in the mesa."

"Spirits?"

"Living men."

"How do you know this?"

"Nakipa told me," she said. "And once, when the moon was full and white, I went to the sacred pool in the canyon and I saw them come down to the water and drink. I ran away."

"The ancient ones live?" Ki shook his head. The remnants of an ancient people, pyramid builders, carvers of stone, people from deep within Mexico, pushed out by the conquistadores. A people with no name, no history, their origins shrouded in the mists of time.

"Who else knows this?"

"Only a few. Nakipa and two of the elders. And me. Others of our tribe have seen them, but Nakipa has always told them they were spirits. That is what the old man who befriended him instructed him to say. The ancient ones are fearful of being discovered. The Spanish men chased them from their land. Now they fear all men, especially white men."

"Nakipa told you this?"

"He told me this."

Ki started his horse forward again. The others had slowed and were looking back from the crest of a sandy rise. He waved an arm to show he was all right.

"Gentle Night—the ancient ones, where do they live?"

"In the mesa, or on top of it, perhaps. Once many years ago I saw smoke there."

Ki looked to the summit of the great mesa. A primitive form itself, perhaps it had drawn the ancient ones. Perhaps also there was a reason besides nature's whims that the Spanish galleon never sailed away again. The ancients despised the Spanish. If there had been a great cavern in the mesa, one carved by the running river, wouldn't they have been capable of closing it?

They could have watched the great ship sail up the Colorado and grown more afraid. Seeing armor and cannon—if they knew what cannon were—seeing Spanish colors, seeing the ship, seemingly a hunting, pillaging thing, sail right toward their sacred refuge, they might have felt stark, cold fear.

And then when the ship had moored inside the great cavern, perhaps the ancients had seen their chance to destroy it. A landslide, perhaps, triggered by some means . . .

It was all uncertain, but it gave Ki much to think about. He lifted his eyes again to the mesa and watched it closely, like a man looking for distant, meaningful smoke.

Riding ahead of Ki and Gentle Night, Andojar also looked to the mesa. He also looked for smoke. He rose nearer to Jessie. He liked the way her breasts jiggled as she rode, the way her bottom fitted the saddle of her roan, the way her honey-blonde hair drifted in the wind.

"We could still turn back," he said.

"Turn back?" She laughed. "Not likely, mister."

"You don't know what's up ahead. I do."

"Santana?"

"Santana and all of his cutthroats, scabs upon the face of the earth. I know," he said wryly. "Most of them I recruited myself."

"Ki and I have been in rough company before."

"Maybe. But you haven't met any like these boys. They kill if they can, and they'll enjoy it. If they ever got hold of you, Jessie . . ."

"All right. I think I know what you're saying. I'm aware of the danger, but I'm not going back."

"I didn't think you would, really."

"What happened?" Jessie asked after a minute. "What made you leave the bandits?"

"What would you like me to tell you? That I had a religious experience, like my father? I know your question is serious, Jessie, but there is no real answer. I lived with violence. I saw it done. I incited it. One day I understood life and no longer understood death. I wanted things which lived to be free to flourish. I did not want carnage on my conscience.

"I picked Santana up in Durango. A scarred, frightened man with oily eyes. When I put a gun in his hand, it was as if I had created him, and so I became a sort of god to Santana. A god, but not one to which he would listen when the gun was in his hand. Then the gun became his god. And when he wanted to kill..."

"Who was it?" Jessica asked.

"The last one?" Andojar was thoughtful. "A woman. A young woman who would not take his insults at a cantina in Paso Robles. She threw a pitcher of beer at his head and cursed him. Santana shot her. Through the hip. Very painful, crippling. We argued and I told him to leave. He laughed and said didn't I know the *bandidos* were on his side, that I was too soft for them, that we had shied away from many rich jobs because of that.

"I couldn't believe it, no," Andojar said, "but when Santana left, the men went with him. They burned down Paso Robles on their way out. I stood in the middle of the fiery street, watching. Then I left and did not return. Until now, when I discovered that Santana was bothering the Napai, my people."

"How did you find out?" Jessie asked. "How did you

know that your father had written us? Who we were?"

"The one-eyed man in my father's rectory. He is an uncle. He tells me everything that happens. He wrote me to tell me."

They were near enough to the mesa for it to shade their bodies. It seemed twice its height, twice its breadth. Red, primitive, monolithic. Jessie could see scrub juniper higher on its flanks now. There were ledges at various heights, but nothing that seemed contiguous enough to provide a way up.

The caprock was half a mile above them; it may as well have been on the moon. She looked carefully for any sign of a cave, but saw nothing suggesting one.

"There is a small valley a little way on. We can camp there for tonight. No fire, of course."

"How near are we to Santana's camp?"

"If they are still in the old camp, too near. Within three miles."

Jessie bit her lower lip and nodded. She turned to look back at Ki and Gentle Night and then beside her, toward Father Carrillo, grim and silent, that primitive, deadly weapon slung over his shoulder.

"They won't find this valley?"

"The *bandidos* are lazy men. After dark they want to drink and sleep, nothing more. We will post a guard anyway, but I would be surprised if they came looking for us. After all," he said with a smile, "why would they expect a small force like this to come looking for Santana? Why, we would have to be insane!"

Behind them now the Indian campfires came to life, red, winking eyes against the subtle purple of dusk on the desert. They would be watching fearfully, holding the children close, gripping their ancient muskets, waiting for the return of Santana.

How long would it be before the cartel got tired of trying to frighten off the Indians and turned to mass slaughter? It wasn't beyond them, Jessie knew. She rode on angry and sober.

They found the little valley higher into the hills, where the mesa itself began to rise. There was a good field of view from the surrounding bluffs. There were oaks in the bottom among huge reddish boulders. There was a little grass for the horses, but no water.

"We'll have to make do with the water bags," Andojar said.

The sun was sinking rapidly now. The flats beyond the hills were deep red. A gold beacon shone through the notch in the far mountains, and then that too was gone.

They ate dried beef and biscuits, drank water from their canteens, and sat together in the silence, knowing that death was a real, waiting thing over the hill.

"We'll have to stand watch," Ki said, rising from the crouch he had eaten in. "I'll go first. Four hours. Then I'll wake whoever will have the second watch."

Father Carrillo shrugged. "Wake me then, Ki."

"I wish you'd take a rifle with you," Andojar told Ki.

"There's no point. Only silence can have any value as a defense against their fifty guns."

"Just be careful," Jessie said.

"I will. Don't sleep close together. Spread yourselves out."

"All right." Jessie looked to the mesa, which blotted out half the evening sky. "It's forbidding, isn't it? Almost alive?"

"It is alive," Ki said. "It trickles dust and seeps water and things live in its entrails. It lives."

He smiled then and was gone into the velvety darkness. The surrounding hills, softened by dusk, were deep violet and gray. Jessie sighed, brushed back her hair, and walked to where her bedroll lay. She was going to sleep—she was going to try to sleep.

The mesa bulked large above them. *Living*.

Ki climbed the bluff to the south and found himself a position where he could observe most of the surrounding area.

It was dark across the desert basin, but moving shadows would catch the eye; the sound of footsteps or a horse's hoof striking a stone would carry for miles; even the dust in the air would indicate movement to a man who kept his senses alert. Ki had little fear of being crept up on.

Until he was.

The shadowy figure was there, nearly beside him, and Ki swung around, dropping into a defensive crouch.

"I have come to be with you," Gentle Night said. "I have come to make you happy."

Chapter 9

"I startled you."

"Yes, go away, woman."

Her hands were on his shirtfront, her eyes were dark and gleaming in the starlight. Ki took her hands away and put them at her side.

"It is not the time for this."

"It is time. My body tells me it is time. Doesn't your body tell you the same, Ki?" Her hands rested on his thighs and then rose to his crotch, cupping him. "I feel the swelling here, the strength of your urge. Feel the living thing which wants to enter my spread body and fill me with its warm need."

"And if you put your hand on my belly, perhaps you would feel my stomach growl. That does not mean I'm going to rush down to eat."

"You have already eaten, though. This other thing I think you have not allowed yourself to do for a time. This, I think, is an even stronger hunger. Feel him . . ." she pressed both of her cupped hands to his crotch, feeling Ki's erection come to life. "He strains against your pants. He wishes to be free. Let him come to me, Ki. Join your need to mine and let us satisfy each other."

Gentle Night's fingers moved to Ki's trouser buttons and began undoing them. He started to stop her and then just rested his hands on her head. His pants were down suddenly and she knelt beside him, placing his swollen member to her cheek, cooing to it, talking to it, her breath warm against his body. Her lips ran along his inner thigh.

"Down," she whispered. "Down, now," and Ki saw her throw her dress over her head. She wore nothing underneath.

The starlight revealed her trim, sleek body. Firm, pointed breasts with taut dark nipples, flat abdomen, smooth dark thighs with a black triangle of mystery between them.

"Come." Gentle Night spread her dress and knelt on it, looking back at Ki. She smiled and leaned forward so that her head rested on her forearms. "Come," she said again, and one hand reached back and spread the soft folds of flesh between her legs.

Ki sank to his knees, kissing her buttocks, his hands roaming her body. She found his shaft and guided him in as Ki knelt behind her, feeling her warmth, the dampness of her. She lifted her head toward the starry sky and her mouth opened in a soundless cry of pleasure as Ki stroked in and out, her fingers touching his shaft.

He hunched forward, groping for her breasts, finding them as Gentle Night became a wild and needful thing swaying against him, her buttocks thudding softly against his pelvis. She began to moan softly, as softly as the night. Sweat stood out on Ki's forehead. Her body was slick and warm, smooth. She began to come undone, her inner muscles going slack and then firm, her entire body shuddering. The head of Ki's shaft was a knot of throbbing nerve endings. He tried to hold Gentle Night motionless, knowing that he would come if she caught him right just one more time.

She couldn't be held back. Their bodies had needs, and they rose to those needs of their own volition. There was nothing at all the mind could do to restrain them, and they met in a wild melee of want, of thrust and sway, until, with his own silent cry filling his throat, Ki leaned back and filled her with his completion.

Gentle Night swayed on for a time until slowly she sagged to the ground and turned over, and Ki, trembling a little, went down with her to kiss her breasts, her abdomen, her shoulders before snuggling to her, smelling the woman scent about her, the yarrow soap in her hair, feeling her stroke the muscles of his back.

"Cute," the man's voice said. "Isn't it cute, Red?"

Ki sat up, reaching for a *shuriken,* but it was already too late. The two men hovered over them, the yellow-haired man in a sombrero and the big redheaded one with the two black eyes. The man from the train.

"You don't know how cute," Red said, and he stepped in and kicked Ki in the face. Ki's head spun around. Blood filled his mouth. Gentle Night's scream was echoing in his ears. The sound of it followed him all the way down a long dark tunnel into the heart of the dark and silent earth.

Jessie's head came around. She stopped on the rise, grabbing Andojar's arm. "It's Ki. Something's happened."

She started toward the sound of the cry, but Andojar grabbed her shoulder.

"No, Jessie."

"They have Ki!"

"We can do nothing now."

"I'm damn sure going to try," she said.

"Yes!" Andojar hissed. "But not now. Not by rushing into their guns. Think, Jessie. Stop for a moment."

He felt her strain against his grip and then felt her body

slacken as she realized that he was right. She nodded.

"All right."

"Okay." He was breathing heavily. They hadn't come far or fast, but there was much tension in the air. It had been Andojar's idea to scout out the Santana camp while the others slept. Jessie hadn't approved.

"I'm going with you," she had insisted.

"It's too dangerous."

"This is all dangerous, for God's sake. Living is dangerous."

"I just want to have a look. I'll be able to spot their fires a long way off."

"And then what?"

"Nothing. I'll be back."

"You still haven't got that crazy idea about killing Santana man to man, stopping things that way?"

He didn't answer. He didn't need to. "I'm going on ahead."

"Not alone, Andojar."

In the end he had given up; he had no choice. If there was another woman as stubborn as Jessie Starbuck around, Andojar had never encountered her.

"Then come with me. But not my father."

"All right."

"He's not cut out for this. He belongs in his church, giving communion."

"I'm not arguing with you," Jessie had said.

"He needs his rest."

"All right."

Then later they had crept from the camp. They had reached the top of the hill behind the camp when they heard the cry from across the valley.

They both went to their bellies in the brush. Jessie saw them then. Six men and ten horses winding up the hillside.

There was something familiar about the first man, the big-shouldered one.

Andojar touched her shoulder and then gestured for silence. Jessie nodded, although her Colt was in her hand and she believed she could have picked off three of the *bandidos* before they knew what hit them.

She could have picked them off, but she and Andojar would likely have been killed—and the prisoners, certainly. Prisoners, for that was what Ki, Gentle Night, and Father Carrillo were. Ki, unconscious, had been slung over the back of the gray gelding, his ankles tied beneath the horse's belly to his wrists. Gentle Night was behind him, her hands tied behind her back. Father Carrillo, his head hanging as if he was suffering terrible pain, rode a paint horse on the far side of the outlaws.

Jessie watched them go by and felt anger and fear mingle in her breast. Andojar was silent, stiff with undefined emotion. They waited until there was nothing left but the scent of dust in the desert night.

"Do we go now?" Jessie asked.

"I go. You're staying. Or better yet, riding back to the mission."

"Now that the joking's out of the way, what are we going to do?" Jessie asked.

"I mean it. I want you to go back."

"I mean it too. I'm not going."

Andojar's sigh was massive. He knew he wasn't going to convince her. Not this one.

"All right. We'll have a look and see what we can do. It should be easy to get close to their camp. They won't suspect there are more of us."

"If they stopped to count bedrolls, they will," Jessie reminded him. Those had been spread out, however, and Santana's men were very likely too lazy to look. Most outlaws are lazy—it's what leads them into their line of work, figuring that stealing is easier than working. They tend to forget that living is usually considered preferable to dying.

"Come on," Andojar said in some annoyance. "I know a way to that camp that few of this bunch will remember, along the side of the mesa...Jessie?"

"What?"

"I hate to have you in danger, maybe it makes me angry with you momentarily, but you are the most woman I have ever known. I care for you."

"I know you do." She stretched up on tiptoe and kissed him briefly. Then she gestured with her revolver. "Let's go."

The pale moon had begun to rise now. Long, crooked shadows crept out from under the thorny mesquite along the ridge. The mesa was black as sin, silent. They rounded a bend in the trail that Andojar was following, and saw the campfires below them.

They paused. Andojar looked at Jessie and started on. The trail wound up the flank of the mesa. It was narrow and crumbling, hardly safe even in daylight, and treacherous by moonlight, but it offered a view down into the outlaw camp.

There weren't so many men as there should have been. A dozen or so were visible. Looking farther south, along the base of Mesa Grande, Jessie could see another fire. It appeared tinier, but it must have been quite a bit larger. She pointed it out to Andojar, who nodded.

The trail ended at a little declivity farther along. The path crumbled away, washed out by flash floods. The floods had formed the narrow canyon below, and now Jessie and Andojar started down it, hidden from view, toward the low rise that flanked the outlaw camp. With Andojar's little trick, they had circled the camp without being seen.

The wash ended in a narrow alluvial fan where boulders lay scattered. They worked their way through these toward the edge of the rise. The moon peered over the hills and into the camp, illuminating most of it.

It was difficult to see what was going on. The cry of pain drifted clearly to them, however, and Jessie's grip on her pistol tightened until her knuckles cracked.

It wasn't Ki. It hadn't been Ki's voice. For some reason, the *bandidos* had singled out Father Carrillo for punishment.

Jessie looked at Andojar, seeing anger engraved on his features. His mouth was a straight line, his jaw clenched. He looked at her and nodded. There was only one way to do this, the direct way. They started down.

Ki shook his head. He couldn't get it cleared. It was filled with flocks of birds, their whirling wings grazing the inside of his skull. Gradually they coalesced into something more solid, real. Pain. Angry, pounding pain that ravaged his brain. He peered through the pain, out at the world where people were making noise, hurting each other, screaming.

"You will leave the girl alone," Father Carrillo said, and grabbed at the redheaded man. "I won't allow you to molest her."

"I'll mo-lest whoever I damn well please, padre." He backhanded the priest violently, and Father Carrillo was knocked to the earth.

Gentle Night was cowering against the sand. Behind her was the fire, blazing brightly, around it six or seven men squatting on their heels, watching the entertainment, drinking tequila and smoking.

Father Carrillo was on his hands and knees, crawling toward the redheaded man, who watched him, hands on hips, upper lip curled back.

The man from the train, Ki's clouded mind decided. And he was going to hurt the priest again. Ki tried to move and discovered he was bound hand and foot. He could do nothing at this point but mutter, "No, Father."

"You will not hurt her..."

The big man kicked Father Carrillo again. First in the head and then in the ribs. The priest cried out in pain and fury. He wanted to get to his feet, to fight, but his numbed body refused him the opportunity.

Ki's own head was clearing. His hands were behind his back, but they were not tied well, and Ki was a master at slipping his bonds. It was a simple matter of temporarily deforming the structure of the hand, of allowing the thumb to free itself, the little finger to actually dislocate briefly. Testing the bonds, Ki could see that it would be an easy task to free himself. What he would be capable of doing then, alone, was another matter.

They heard a horse approaching, heard a man whistle sharply. Heads turned and several of the men at the fire came to their feet.

It was another minute before the bandit leader entered the camp. Ki knew him immediately—not his features, the dark eyes, thin, twisted nose, not the cruel mouth, but he knew the type. He knew a madman when he saw one.

"What is all this?" Santana swung down from his horse, which was tricked out in silver. He wore a red shirt with ballooning sleeves above black jeans, and carried two tied-down pistols; a black sombrero with a silver band shadowed his face.

"We found them over the hill. A priest, a Chinaman, and a girl."

"Kill them." Santana turned away, leading his horse. "Kill the other two first, and let the priest pray for their souls. Then kill him."

"Not the woman!" one of the bandits at the fire objected. Santana turned, his dark, deepset eyes gleaming. He walked to the man and kicked him in the face. He rolled over into the fire, scattering sparks, and crawled away. No one helped him up.

"Santana—" the redhead dared to speak up. *"They* won't like it."

"They can go to hell."

"They are paying us, Santana."

Santana's hand reached tentatively for his gun. His fingers tapped the ivory handle of the right-hand Colt. Then he relaxed and smiled a wide, meaningless, mad smile.

"Maybe you are right, Gore. Eh, maybe he is right, *caballeros*. Maybe the men in the black suits want to see these people, to talk to them. What can they tell us, Gore?"

"I don't know," the red-haired man said, "but they must have a reason for coming here. Everyone knows Santana is camped here. No one would come without a good reason."

"Ask the priest."

That was a problem. Father Carrillo couldn't speak. Gore had been a little too exuberant.

"The girl, then."

"Maybe we should leave this to the—"

"Ask the girl!" Santana shrieked.

"What are you doing here, girl?" Gore asked Gentle Night in English. There was no answer. Gore tried Spanish. "Come on, girl," he said, twisting her chin around, "what are you doing here?"

She answered with a stream of abuse in her own tongue, the Napai tongue. Gore looked around and shrugged. "How about you, China boy?" The big man smiled, and it was an evil smile. In his hand Ki saw the skinning knife which he had slipped from inside his boot. "Don't tell me you don't speak English—I heard you on the train. Remember that?

When you got a little rough with me. I owe you some, China boy. What are you doing here?"

"I will tell your masters, dog," Ki said, "but not you."

"My masters! Them foreign, struttin' bastards!" Gore was genuinely furious. "They might pay me, they might tell me what to do, but—"

"Gore." Santana's voice was remarkably soft. He stood over Ki, his eyes gleaming. "Ask him again. If he does not answer, open his throat."

"Did you hear, China boy? And you know damn well it'll give me pleasure to do it."

"Ki!" Gentle Night cried out.

Gore glanced at her, then asked, "What are you doing here? Are you alone, the three of you? Who sent you?"

The knife point touched Ki's neck, and Gore pushed a little harder, drawing a fine trickle of blood.

"What are you doing here?"

Ki didn't get the chance to consider an answer. The pistols opened up from the edge of the camp and the night exploded into noise and flame.

Chapter 10

Andojar's first shot took one of the men by the fire and kicked him back into it, where he lay sizzling. His second was aimed at Santana. An off-handed shot fired from the left-handed pistol, it missed and Santana, swinging up behind his horse, fired back, sending Andojar to the ground in a long dive.

Jessie's double-action Colt fired three times. Two of the shots scored hits. A *bandido* waking from a drunken sleep grabbed for his rifle and started to bring it up, and Jessie tagged him with a .38 slug in the chest.

Recognizing Gore, she tried for the redheaded man next. Her bullet struck flesh low on the leg, and Gore howled with pain but didn't seem badly hurt.

Ki had been in motion from the first shot. Shrugging the bonds from his wrists, he grabbed the skinning knife Gore had dropped in the excitement and cut his ankles free.

Gore, hit in the leg, had begun hobbling toward his horse, firing over his shoulder. Ki started after him, but ran into a rifle-wielding *bandido*. With one swinging kick, Ki knocked the Winchester from the bandit's hands and, continuing through, struck the point of his chin, knocking him unconscious.

There were still four or five bandits fighting back, although Santana had fled and Gore had disappeared. Ki saw them leveling a barrage of rifle fire at the small depression where Jessie and Andojar had taken cover.

From the corner of his eye, Ki saw the priest dragging himself toward the pile of captured belongings taken from Ki's party. The monstrous four-barreled shotgun lay there, and as Ki watched, four eight-gauge shells were loaded into the terrible thundergun.

When it went off, one barrel after another, it was like the roar of a mountain storm, thunder and lightning filling the night. The bandits were blown in all directions, pieces of them scattered across the sand as the cloud of smoke the scattergun had belched out slowly drifted away.

"Holy Mary," the priest said, and crossed himself.

Ki walked to where Gentle Night sat, astonished and stunned. He helped her to her feet and she clung to him briefly. Jessie and Andojar walked into the camp, which was strewn with the dead like a battlefield when the guns have been silenced.

"Are you all right?" Jessie asked. She looked into Ki's eyes as she asked him. She smiled and touched his cheek.

"Yes, but I fear we are in even more danger now. Santana will be back with the bulk of his men. We can't be so lucky again."

"Where, then? Back to the mission?" Gentle Night said.

"And what will that solve?" Jessie asked. She was reloading her Colt. "We're into this up to our necks. Even if we go back to the mission, they'll follow and maybe burn the mission down, maybe slaughter the mission Indians."

Andojar agreed. "Jessie is right. All we can do is go on."

"Toward death?" Carrillo asked.

"We all go on toward death, do we not, Father?"

The priest nodded. "Yes. Yes, we do."

"You?" Andojar asked when he was half turned away. "Are you all right, Father?"

"I am all right."

"You've taken a terrible beating. You're not young any longer."

"No, I am not young."

Andojar nodded. *"Bueno."* He looked at the dead, thinking perhaps of Santana, who had gotten away, or giving names to the *bandidos,* men he had known once. "We had better hurry on, I think."

"Which way?" Ki asked.

It was Jessie who answered. "Toward their fire. Toward their other camp. I want to know what they're doing up ahead, don't you?"

"Walk into their camp again!"

"Again. If we can't go back, that only leaves forward."

"She is right, of course," Ki said.

"I suggest, then," Gentle Night said, "that we go now. I can hear horses approaching."

They had their own horses there, but they decided to leave them and go ahead on foot. Jessie looked at the dead again. There were a lot of horses in that camp with no riders.

They started out into the desert, circling wide of the camp. They were leaving tracks, but in the darkness, even with a moon, it would take a skilled man to follow them. Santana probably didn't have much use for a tracker—his gang ran more to cutthroats and sadists.

They saw the gang's horses, shadowy things rising from the sand, and went to the ground to lie there watching, waiting until Santana's men rode by.

Jessie had seen the silver-mounted saddle, the silver hat-band, and it had been a temptation just to kill him, to finish the bastard, but it would have done no one any good, as she had managed to convince Andojar.

When the dust had settled, they started on, more hurriedly, over the broken hills toward the fiery glow to the south. Carrillo was limping and his face was purpled and swollen, but he seemed to be managing. If Ki was hurt, he didn't say anything. Jessie herself felt only tired and thirsty, but her dry mouth may have been from the excitement, and a little from fear.

Ki hissed through his teeth and motioned with both hands. They dropped to their bellies and crawled to the top of the sandy rise.

Below them, a fire blazed away, revealing a bizarre sight. Dozens of men, some of them apparently Indian slaves, worked by the light of the fire—three fires, actually—carrying stone away from a massive excavation in the side of the mesa. Around them stood half a dozen *bandidos* with crossed arms or Winchesters held at the ready, watching.

"What are they doing? My God!"

"Moving a mountain. Looking for a river."

"Madness."

"Not considering the stakes. Those galleons carried uncounted millions of gold. From a land where everything seemed to be made of gold, where it seemed limitless and the conquerors took all there was."

Jessie looked at Ki. If there had been the slightest doubt that the cartel was involved in this, there was none now. No one else would have the resources, the audacity, the calculated cruelty necessary to pull off an operation like this.

"What do we do?" Andojar asked. "Start shooting?"

"No," Jessie said. "Two things. First, find the leaders.

Cut off the head of this operation. The men in dark suits."

"And the second?"

"Find the galleon."

"When they cannot? With all their labor?"

"Maybe there's another way in. There has to have been a way out. Once. The map got out."

"Perhaps later there was another cave-in."

That was possible too. Jessie didn't know. She shrugged.

"What do you want to do, then?" Andojar whispered.

"Let's have a closer look," she answered. Ki silently agreed. He looked a little grim, but Jessie saw him still his breath, calm himself, prepare himself for what lay ahead.

They started down the darkened slope toward the excavation.

Above, the mesa tilted toward them. Immutable, indomitable. There were small noises deep within it, like the humming of a beehive. It might have been the workers, or it could have been the spirits of the ancients, the restless souls of the lost conquistadores who had come to a strange land to die, never to see Spain and family again.

The guard turned his head at the wrong moment, and when he looked back, half blinded by the firelight, it was too late. Ki was behind him, striking like a panther, silent and efficient. Pressure on the main nerves of the man's neck put the guard out, and Ki quickly slipped the jacket and torn, greasy sombrero from the body.

He grimaced as he put the filthy jacket on, putting the guard's bandolier over his shoulder, picking up his rifle.

They started on through the shadows, seeing the Indian slaves with their barrows and sledges dragging or rolling stones from the excavation, which appeared larger and larger as they neared it. Jessie could see, near the top of the cave, older, time-cut formations. The cartel had found the entrance to the cavern.

A second guard appeared out of the darkness. He peered at Ki, who was walking behind Jessie and Gentle Night with his rifle, as if guarding them.

"*Qué pasa?*" The guard got closer to Ki, fell back startled as he recognized that something was wrong, and went down in a heap as Ki slammed the edge of his hand into his neck.

Father Carrillo grabbed this one's hat and serape, and they moved on.

The cave mouth was before them. Huge, firelit, vast. Voices echoed through it. Men labored and grunted with exertion.

There was a set of rails running from the interior of the cave, a mine cart sitting at the end of the tracks. They hadn't come to do half a job. If there was gold there, they meant to find it.

There was much water underfoot as they started warily into the cavern. They had tapped the underground river, and it was flowing out onto the desert. Torches were set at intervals along the walls now. Jessie took one from its iron holder and carried it with her.

They worked toward the back of the cavern, following a narrow path that wound slightly upward along the cavern wall. Below, they could see the ore carts rumbling along the rails. A man shouted something indistinct as iron struck iron. There was much rubble lying about. The water was two feet on the far side of the tracks.

"How far?"

"As far as we can go."

"Do you hear that? Picks. We're nearly there."

They went ahead, nearing the sounds of work. Now Jessie began to see tunnels leading off to the sides of the large shaft—tunnels that must have gone nowhere, since otherwise the cartel would have used them. Tunnels that wound up and down, twisting through the heart of the mesa.

"It's rotten inside," Jessie noted. "The whole darn thing's honeycombed."

"Water," Andojar said. "Water and much, much time."

They rounded a bend in the trail, ducked low to clear a ledge of gray stone, and were suddenly there. Men worked at a wall of stone thirty feet high, stone that had crumbled and fallen and blocked off the immense cavern behind it. They were mainly Indians, these laborers, with a few whites. Around them, more armed guards watched with dark, hostile eyes.

And standing on a narrow ledge above the workers were two men in dark suits and dark hats. Jessie nudged Ki, but he had already seen them. His eyes glittered with ferocity; his head hung slightly forward.

"Yes," Jessie whispered, "I would like to get my hands on their throats, as well."

They waited there in the shadows, watching as the slave-labor gang cleared away the old cave-in.

Did they feel eyes upon them? Perhaps it was the torch in a place it didn't belong, or some slight sound, but slowly, very slowly, one of the cartel men turned his head and looked directly at Jessie. He nudged the other, who looked that way too, before Jessie could pull back.

"Get her!" The voice echoed and boomed in the cavern as the stubby white pointing finger came up. "That is *Starbuck!* Get her!"

Ki saw the pointing finger and then was forced to the ground as the first shots rang out. He was groping for a *shuriken*—it was a long throw, but worth the try—but the guns drove him back. Andojar was firing back, as was Gentle Night, with her newly acquired repeater.

A guard charged up the slope toward them, and took a bullet in the belly. He was punched back over the side of the trail to land sprawled on the stone below. Jessie fired at a man to her left and ducked behind a pillar of stone as she missed and the guard returned her fire. Bullets whined off the stone above and behind them, showering them with rock dust and splinters of stone.

Jessie sighted her Colt and squeezed off again. The guard was hit hard, turned and knocked backward by the .38 bullet. He fell headfirst into the newly born river.

The Indians stood watching in disbelief, in fear. They ducked behind piles of rubble and behind the ore carts as the guards opened up in earnest.

"Let's get the hell out of here!" Andojar shouted. He was firing with both hands, but there was too much fire-power below.

"Where!"

There was nowhere to go, really. Back toward the main entrance where there were more guards, where a returning Santana might be waiting.

"A side tunnel!" Jessie shouted.

"No! It might be a dead end," Ki answered.

Bullets peppered the stone walls around them, ricocheting off into the cavern vastness, pinging away as their force dwindled. The roar of the guns echoed and rechoed savagely, deafeningly.

"I'm hit," Father Carrillo cried out. Blood was leaking from his arm, his shirt had been clipped away neatly by a bullet, and now through that narrow cut blood flowed copiously, drenching his sleeve.

"Let's get out of here!" Jessie said again. Gentle Night was tying a tourniquet above the priest's gunshot wound. It was all any of them could do, but it wouldn't help much.

"There's no choice," Andojar said. He was rapidly thumbing cartridges into his Colts. The outlaws took advantage of the temporary lull to rush up the slope.

Jessie saw the thundergun lying on the floor of the cavern

and she snatched it up, cocking all four hammers. When she triggered it, the world seemed to go up in smoke and flame. She was slammed to her seat by the recoil of the shotgun. Her ears rang and roared. Her shoulder felt broken. Five outlaws lay dead or wounded below.

"Come on." Ki took her hand and lifted her to her feet. Jessie shook her head, but the echoing ringing wouldn't clear. Ki was saying something, but it was a while before it got through. "Move! Let's go, Jessie—there are more of them on the way."

They started toward the feeder tunnel, Gentle Night, helping Father Carrillo, lead the way, followed by Ki and Jessie with Andojar bringing up the rear, occasionally returning fire from the pursuing guards.

There were four tunnels in a row to their left, all water-carved, low. Gentle Night started up the first one they came to, but for some reason Jessie called out, "No!" and they went on to the next, hoping that her instincts were right.

Jessie had picked up the fallen torch, and now, with a pistol in one hand and the torch in the other, she went ahead of Gentle Night and into the tunnel. The stone was black, polished, the ceiling of varying heights. It wound slightly down and to their right. The torchlight danced eerily across the smooth, undulating ceiling.

"I hope you've chosen the right way," Andojar said. His voice reverberated through the tunnel. Jessie glanced back and winked.

She heard the distant shot, heard the echoes, but still she was amazed when the whining ricochet whipped past them, ringing along like a stone thrown through a pipe. If the guards fired enough rounds, chance was going to bring them down eventually. With any luck, the *bandidos* wouldn't realize that. There was nothing to do but hurry on and fire an occasional warning shot behind them.

The tunnel began to narrow. The ceiling was lower, so that they had to move on in a crouch. There were no sounds now but their labored breathing and the occasional sob of pain from Father Carrillo. Jessie moved more slowly now, thrusting the torch in front of her, not knowing what to expect ahead. They could run head-on into a band of outlaws coming the other way. If that happened, they would be caught in a murderous crossfire.

What did happen was just as bad. They rounded a tight bend in the tunnel and came to a dead end. Jessie turned, her arms outstretched, her teeth clenched, and she muttered an apology. She had brought them all this way to die in the heart of Mesa Grande. Behind them they could hear the pounding of boots. The pursuit was drawing nearer, and there was just nothing they could do about it. Nothing at all.

Chapter 11

"Up," Ki said, and they looked to him. His eyes were raised and he pointed toward the ceiling. There was a narrow fissure of some sort visible in the stone, not more than a foot or two wide. "We'll have to go up."

"Up to what?" Andojar said in frustration.

"I don't know. It's better than waiting here to die."

"Yes." Andojar looked back down the tunnel behind them. "Up, then. I will have a look."

"No. Let me," Ki said. He looked up again, and they saw him give his head a little shake. They could hear the boots again, louder, and voices. "You'd better let them know we're here," Ki said.

Andojar drew a pistol and fired four times in rapid succession down the stony corridor behind them. A man cried out in pain and they heard the footsteps retreat. Only one shot was fired in retaliation, but it died on the way, ricocheting its way to oblivion.

"It is bad," Andojar heard Gentle Night say. He turned to see that the women were crouched over his father, then turned his eyes away deliberately.

"Give them another shot or two in a minute," Ki said. "I think they will not be in a hurry." He added soberly, "They know we have chosen a dead-end tunnel."

"Thanks to me," Jessie said.

"Whatever is was meant to be," Ki said. It wasn't very comforting. He had been studying the fissure for a long minute. Now he reached up, took a grip on something inside the cleft, and drew himself up. "Andojar?" he said, and the man in black gave him a slight boost. Then Ki's feet vanished and he was gone.

He inched upward through the cold darkness, feeling his way. It was impossible to see anything and impossible to carry a torch, and so he groped his way upward.

His hand slipped and he nearly fell. Water was seeping over the smooth stone. The walls of the fissure, instead of opening wider, were drawing together. Ki had to exhale, relaxing his chest before he could drag himself upward an inch at a time toward whatever lay above.

Sweat had begun to run from his forehead. His hands and knees were raw. After the constricted section he had just traversed, the tunnel seemed to widen out, and now, reaching up as far as he could, Ki found a ledge of sorts. How wide it was he couldn't tell, but it offered a decent momentary grip. He hung there for a time, panting. The darkness was close and heavy. He could hear distant, muffled sounds, like many voices speaking in unison.

Ki chinned himself and threw a knee up tentatively. His leg went over onto the ledge and he rolled up. It was wide, surprisingly so. He couldn't see into the blackness to know just how wide it was. He touched a stone wall, felt the dampness there, and moved forward very slowly, finding a sudden gap, an opening.

There was another tunnel mouth then—leading off into the unknown, into further darkness. Ki went back to the ledge and started down again. He heard a flurry of shots from below and hurried on.

Dropping to the floor of the tunnel, he found himself face to face with Jessie and Andojar.

"Well?" Jessie asked expectantly.

"There's a way out."

"What are we waiting for?" Andojar said.

"I don't know where it goes—if anywhere."

"We know where staying here leads," Andojar said. They looked back down the corridor behind them.

"Your father can't make it much farther."

"He'll make it. I'll carry him if I have to."

"No." The voice was weak, strangled. They looked to where Father Carrillo lay, blood seeping from his wounds. "I can't go on..."

"Father..."

"And don't try to make me. I can prevent them from following you. Give me my thundergun."

"Father Carrillo, please," Ki began, but the priest waved a hand.

"Leave me alone. Let me have the comfort of sitting here, of knowing that I am helping somehow. I am ready to go to my Maker. I have things to answer for, but I am ready nevertheless."

"Ki?" Jessie asked.

"A man has the right to choose his own way," Ki replied.

Gentle Night stood watching. Now she cocked her head and said, "They come again—silently. I can hear their footsteps."

Andojar was at his father's side. He knelt down now, and wiped back a strand of gray hair from the priest's eye.

"Andojar," Carrillo said, "forgive me. I was only a man."

"Forgive me," Andojar replied. "For I was only a boy." And then the outlaw bowed his head and kissed the priest's cheek. He stood, too hastily, and said sharply, "All right, then, let us go. Quickly!"

Three shots sounded from behind them. Andojar fired back blindly, emptying both of his pistols down the corridor like rolling thunder. The corridor was filled with smoke and sound when his hammers finally fell on empty chambers.

He turned and looked at them. "Now can we go?"

Jessie looked back at Father Carrillo sitting on the floor of the cavern tunnel, the thundergun across his lap. He looked pale, shrunken, but at peace and quite alert.

"Goodbye," she said, then she started up the cleft behind Ki, who was leading the way.

They reached the ledge a long ten minutes later, just as the awful roar of the four-barrel shotgun reached them from below.

And then dead silence.

"Come on," Ki said. They looked at him. By the feeble torchlight his expression was taut, grave.

"Do you know where you're taking us?"

"Perhaps nowhere at all. Father Carrillo has given us some time to look, to grope our way along. There must be another way out somewhere."

Not necessarily, Jessie thought, but didn't say. They started forward. The torchlight showed a ledge perhaps thirty feet long by twenty wide. An oddly formed knob of stone hung from the ceiling like a lamp. Beyond that there was a narrow tunnel mouth, leading into the unknown.

Ki led the way, ducking low to enter the tunnel. The firelight flashed their shadows, huge and writhing, against the walls of the tunnel, which opened and began to slant downward.

Jessie moved cautiously but rapidly in Ki's footsteps. The tunnel made another downward twist and then opened onto a spectacular and massive cavern. Jessie's breath caught.

Limestone stalactites and stalagmites like a dragon's teeth

yawned at them from out of the darkness. Above them they could see water trickling from another tunnel mouth, falling fifty feet in a narrow waterfall. Beyond that, a dozen or two dozen more tunnel mouths of different shapes and sizes showed like a wasp's nest or a broken honeycomb.

"It's rotten," Andojar said. "The entire mesa is nothing but caves. What's holding it up?"

Time and water had worked their will on Mesa Grande. It stood hollow, eroded, magnificent outside, a shell inside.

As they stood staring out at the vast open cavern, rock crumbled from beneath Jessie's feet.

"A labyrinth," Ki said. "What will we do?"

"We can't go back."

"Nor can we go on, unless we know which way to go."

"We'll just have to choose a way," Andojar said irritably. "I'm not going to stand here in the darkness and wait to die."

"Nor am I," Ki said. "I only wanted to point out that there was a choice. Jessie? Do we go on?"

"There's no choice," she answered. "I think we all know what will happen if we stop."

"All right." Ki looked around. "Which way, then?"

"Down."

They started downward. The ceiling of the great vault was a hundred feet above them now. Bluish gargoyles stared down from the walls, odd time- and water-formed stone creatures haunting every ledge and nook.

Ki suddenly vanished. He was there and then he wasn't. They heard him cry out and Jessie saw him fall. She rushed forward. Andojar behind her. He was clinging to his fingertips to a ridge of stone. Below, a vertical shaft dropped away endlessly. Stone trickled away from beneath his feet, and it was a long, long time before they could hear it hit bottom.

"Get his wrist."

"Up," Jessie said, tugging. "Come on, Ki, quit playing." Her heart was in her throat. He could easily have dropped to the bottom of the shaft, and he would never have come up again alive. They moved on more carefully, Ki taking the torch now as they worked their way through a forest of stalagmites three to four feet thick, cold and pale, like giant sentinels. They could hear water running constantly now, sometimes feel it beneath their feet.

Jessie had given up worrying about the pursuit. The *bandidos* wouldn't be anxious to come after them now. The maze of tunnels was an impossible area to search. Sound echoed endlessly. It wasn't likely that anyone could sneak up on them—it was more likely that they were back there laughing their heads off at Jessie and Ki, knowing that they were lost in the bowels of the mountain, lost hopelessly.

They had come to another dead end. Ki wiped the perspiration from his eyes. It was cold in the cavern, but sweat rained from his head. His shirt stuck to his back. His eyes were gritty from staring out at the cave by torchlight.

"Which way?"

"Is there a way?"

Ki pointed. "Up there, another cave opening. Below, you see—there—another way."

"I don't know," Jessie answered. "Downward, I suppose."

"Andojar?"

"Downward. The top of the mesa is half a mile up. I don't think there's any hope of ever reaching it if you don't know what you're doing."

Gentle Night hadn't given an opinion. Ki looked at her now, seeing rapt attention on her face.

"What is the matter?"

"Don't you hear it?" the Indian girl asked.

"Hear what?"

"Listen."

"I don't hear anything," Jessie said after a minute.

"Nor I," Andojar said. "Why are we standing here? Let's move along."

"But I hear them," Gentle Night said. She gripped Ki's arm tightly. "I hear them, Ki. The voices."

"The *bandidos?*"

She laughed. "No! Not them. Spirit voices. The voices of the ancient ones, the haunted ones. They are in here with us now."

"The girl's crazy," Andojar said. He was tired and angry. He was in no mood for ghost stories. "There's nothing here but us and the damnable darkness and the *bandidos.*" And that, he thought, was enough.

They started down the little corridor, which sloped away from the floor of the big cavern. It was there that they found the skull.

Jessie was working her way along the narrowing path. The stone was crumbling away beneath her feet, and when she put out her hand to brace herself, she touched a hidden recess in the stone wall.

She didn't scream—Jessie was made of tougher stuff than that, and she had seen too much of death in her life to have it affect her like that—but she felt her breath catch, and her body stiffened in that position—arm outstretched, legs slightly bent, head thrown back.

"What is it?" Andojar wanted to know. Jessie pointed.

In the recess sat a human skull, staring blindly back from out of the lost centuries. There was no jawbone, only the grimacing yellow skull, its eye sockets huge and dark. Firelight moved across the skull and seemed to give it the expression of flesh. It leered and mocked and scorned.

"A skull."

"Another lost traveler."

"Who put his own head in a niche in the wall?" Jessie asked, looking at Andojar, who was attempting a smile for her sake.

"What is it?" Ki asked. Then he too saw the skull.

"An ancient one," Gentle Night said.

"Maybe so."

Andojar asked, "An Indian, lost in this cavern?"

"Perhaps. And some sort of burial ritual. Who knows what the ancient ones believe in."

"Do they believe in murder?" Jessie asked.

"What?"

"Look here. There's a hole in the back of the skull. Behind the ear."

"That was no accident."

Andojar had found something else. Crouching, he picked it up.

It glittered softly in his hand. Ki and Jessie watched as his hand raised it toward their eyes. It was a doubloon, glittering, gleaming, shining still after all this time. Gold never loses its luster.

"Sixteenth century," Andojar said.

"Did it—" Ki interrupted himself. "Behind the skull," he said. "What is that?"

He reached in himself, and as something small scuttled away, he picked up the metal object. It was a helmet. Rusted, rotted, dark and time-battered. He turned it over and showed it to them. "He was a Spaniard," Ki commented.

"Then why this sort of burial? Why place his head in the alcove?" Andojar asked.

"He was Spanish. It doesn't follow that his burial was at the hands of Spaniards. Or his murder."

"The ancient ones," Gentle Night said. Her eyes were suddenly fearful. The darkness seemed more intense than ever. "The ancient ones killed him."

"Don't talk nonsense," Andojar snapped.

"It is not nonsense! Who else could it have been?"

"Who else indeed?" Ki said.

"His friends. Thieves fall out. Perhaps too much gold went into this man's pocket."

"All right."

Andojar went on, "Suppose the Indians did kill him—that was centuries ago. It has nothing to do with us. The ancient ones are all gone. Long ago."

Andojar himself didn't look convinced by his argument. They started on again.

The torch was burning low. Sputtering, it hissed and sparked. They had made their torch of rags soaked in coal oil. The flame was steady if smoky and relatively long-lived. But it could only burn for so long. They all began to watch it apprehensively. It was one thing to be lost in a vast cavern with hunters behind and the possibility of starvation and death ahead—but to be without light down here was much worse. It was unthinkable. It was, as they all realized, certain, horrible death. They trudged on as the torch burned lower.

★
Chapter 12

Jessie sagged to the ground. She just sat there. They had decided to halt; all of them were exhausted, and now she let her muscles relax after a long night. Or was it day? There was no telling in the interior of the great cavern.

Gentle Night looked relatively fresh, as did Ki. Jessie and Andojar sat side by side, breathing deeply, watching the torchlight, the vast cave beyond.

They had come to yet another vault, this one with a ceiling fifty feet overhead, with strange alcoves and twisted pillars carved out of the native stone by eons of trickling, seeping water.

"We have to save the torch," Ki said.

"What do you mean?"

"I mean we have to put it out, that's all there is to it."

"He's right," Andojar said. "We'll need it when we start on. We can sleep for an hour or so."

"And when we start on," Gentle Night asked, "where are we going?"

No one had an answer for her. There was nowhere to go. There were only four people in the world, and they inhabited the bowels of the earth, roaming endless corridors eternally. Soon they too would be skulls sitting in niches waiting to be discovered by later explorers; their bones would lie scattered across the cavern floor.

"Put it out," Jessie said.

Ki smothered the torch with his vest, and then the darkness descended. Not a normal darkness, a soft and quiet darkness, but total and complete blackness that rested on the body and mind like a heavy cloak, an oppressive, living thing that breathed in their ears, making vague threats. Jessie rolled close to Andojar and held him.

He turned toward her and clung to her, his lips following the line of her throat to her collarbone, to the upward slope of her soft breasts. Jessie closed her eyes, feeling his fingers slowly unbutton her blouse, his lips grazing her nipples. She lifted her knees and spread them, and Andojar's fingers probed her, finding the soft warmth, the dampness between her smooth thighs.

He shifted slightly and Jessie reached down, finding his solid shaft with her hands. Wrapping her fingers around it, she lifted herself slightly and slipped the head of his erection inside. Just the head, and her inner muscles twisted with anticipation, worked against the knob of flesh that was Andojar in the darkness.

He couldn't wait. He sank into her, feeling her warm moistness envelop him, feeling the pulsing in his loins, the need to fill her, to rock and sway against her, to bite at her breasts, to lift her by her buttocks and drive himself into her until his satisfaction came with an urgent rush.

She reached down, cupping his sack as she whispered into his ear—pretty meaningless words—and Andojar came with a violent bucking, an arching of his back, a loin-draining orgasm.

Jessie lay there unmoving, feeling her own body develop

its climax. It was a softer, quieter climax than Andojar's. He was still in her, still hard. His warmth seeped from her and trickled down her thigh. She could feel her body quiver inside, feel her womb open up and release a rush of satisfaction. Tingling currents ran up from where Andojar filled her, to her breasts, where her nipples stood taut under his ministrations, up her spine and to her fingertips, which still cupped Andojar's heavy sack, lightly touching his healthy manhood.

They slept, and the darkness was washed away briefly. They slept and were warm and the night ceased to become a frightening thing.

Jessie heard the cries first. It was an hour later—or two or three—and she sat upright. Andojar slept beside her still, and now he stirred.

"What is it?"

"I don't know. Listen."

Andojar did so, and then distantly the sounds came to him—perhaps it was a trick of the wind in the cave, or of the water that ran everywhere, but it sounded for all the world like the cries of a man in pain, dreadful pain.

"The ancient ones," Gentle Night said from out of the darkness, and this time no one argued with her.

There was someone there. Someone living in the heart of the dying mesa. Someone who must have lived a molelike existence, a dreadful and strange life.

"It is the wind," Ki said, but he didn't believe it himself. There was no wind, had been no wind, and so far as they knew, there was no way for wind to enter the cavern. "It is the wind," he said again, and then, without discussing it among themselves, they rose and lit the torch and started on.

The trail they had chosen led inexorably downward and they followed it. There was no choice, nowhere else to go.

It wound along the side of the cavern wall now, and the floor of the cave fell away beside them. There was a pit on their right that might have dropped all the way to Hades. They had difficulty breathing. They shuffled forward rather than walking, moving carefully, conserving their strength.

The wild thing popped up in front of them, a tangle of hair falling past his shoulders. In its hand was a pointed stick. They had surprised it trying to strike flint and make a fire. Now it stood facing Andojar, thrusting at him with the stick.

"Don't hurt him!" Ki said loudly, and his voice rang through the cavern. Then the thing rushed at Andojar, trying to drive the pointed stick through his body, and there wasn't any choice.

Ki could have fended off the attack with his bare hands, taken the stick from him and brought him to his knees without hurting him. Andojar didn't have the training necessary for that. When the man drove the stake at his guts, he used the tools he did have, the only tools he had used for years.

The Colt came up and spat angry flame against the darkness. The thing, the wild-haired ancient one—if that was what it was—was hurled backward to slip and stumble before toppling into the bottomless pit beside the trail. The gunshot echoed for a long, long time.

"Damn," Andojar said breathily.

"What was it?"

"*Who*—who was it?"

"I didn't mean to kill him," Andojar said.

"Was it an ancient one, Gentle Night?"

"I don't know," she said. She had never seen one. She had seen shadows and distant figures, like smoke, and she had tended to imagine them as looking like her people did, as she did.

This thing—this hairy creature—couldn't be one of them.

128

But it had to be, didn't it?

"Could he have been Spanish?" Ki asked.

Andojar laughed out loud. "Only if he was over two hundred years old, my friend."

"Not necessarily," Ki answered.

"What are you talking about? Are you mad?"

"Perhaps." Ki seemed to consider that possibility seriously. "I only wondered."

"Descendants of the conquistadores! Of the sailors of the golden galleon!"

"Perhaps," Ki said again. "I only wondered."

"How, Ki?" Jessie asked. "They had no women."

"We don't know that. Men find women wherever they go. There are many Indian women in Mexico."

"That's crazy!" Andojar said. *"If* there were women— if these people were trapped inside the mesa, in this cavern—why, they would all be dead anyway. How could they survive without food, water, air, light, fire, with nothing at all?"

"There is water." Ki picked up the flint that the thing— the man—had been working with. There was a torch there as well, made of fiber bonded somehow to wood. The wood itself was old, very old. "He had fire."

"But they would need food! A man can't survive in darkness, not forever, not all of his life."

"Other creatures do." Ki shrugged again. "I don't know, I only postulate. What else are we to do? I will tell you this—this man knew what fire was. This man knew how to survive in a cave. Could he live here his entire life? If he had to, I suppose. It would not be a long life, not a good life, but with food . . ."

"There are things living here," Gentle Night said. "I have seen the bats. I have seen little white things like lizards without eyes—all white."

"Salamanders," Jessie said. "I've seen them too. They

129

have no eyes. Living in darkness, they have lost their need for them."

"Bats." Andojar shook his head.

"If you had to survive, you would eat them, I don't doubt."

"No. I can't accept this at all. A race of men living in this cavern. They would have found a way out!" He spread his hands. "They would have somehow..." He was quiet. Perhaps there just was no way. The first generation would have tried desperately to get out. But what about the second and the third, which would know no other life, which might even fear light? They would have the traditions of their ancestors, a tradition which said that out there—somewhere—were men pursuing them with guns and cannon. Perhaps they had hidden here and grown accustomed to it, grown to *desire* it!

"It could mean there's no way out at all except the way the cartel has opened up," Jessie said thoughtfully. She was still looking down into the dark pit at her feet, still thinking about the man-thing that had gone to his death there. Out hunting for food, he had run into four strange creatures. Fear must have flashed in his mind—*the hunters had come!* —and he had attacked, only to be killed by a strange and powerful weapon.

"There is a way," Andojar said. "This I know. Somewhere."

"Somewhere."

The trail began to grow narrower, steeper yet. They descended into a corridor where water ran six inches deep. Cold, cold water.

"We're nearly down there," Jessie said.

"Down where?"

"To the source. To the heart of the mountain. To where all of this began."

She could say that with a certainty she didn't understand herself. It went beyond reason, and she knew it with every fiber of her body. This was the seed of the problem, the crux of the mystery.

The water grew deeper, and soon the trail withered away to nothing. There was only the torchlight, the dark stone, the underground river running.

"Which way now?"

"Upstream," Ki said.

"We're more likely to find a way out if we follow the current," Andojar said. He had paused to wipe the sweat from his forehead. The torch in his hand, the man-thing's torch, flared up once and then settled to a smoky glow. The torch Ki carried, the one taken from the cartel's worksite, was nearly out. It hissed and flickered uncertainly.

"Upstream," Ki said. "What do you say, Jessie?"

"Whatever your instincts tell you. It's awfully low up ahead, though," she commented, meaning the roof of the cave, which was less than five feet from the bed of the river.

"Upstream," Ki said positively.

They went upstream, wading through the black icy water while the distant cry of pain continued. It was always there, a haunting thing, a wail, a dirge, a timeless cry out of the darkness. The ceiling lowered. They moved on, bent over at the waist, climbing slightly now. Something grew on the stone beneath the water. Moss or lichen, slippery and treacherous. Twice Jessie went down, tearing skin off her knee the second time.

"What is that?"

Gentle Night stopped. Her dark eyes were wide and searching, as if by staring hard enough she could hear better.

"The crying? I hear it still."

"Not that," she said. "Something else. I don't like this."

131

"What?"

"I don't know. It is alive. It has many eyes."

Jessie and Andojar exchanged a glance. Maybe the closeness of the cave, the darkness, the uncertainty was beginning to prey on Gentle Night's mind. What was she talking about? They asked her again, but she couldn't be more specific.

"I can't hear anything," Andojar said.

"Should we go on, Gentle Night?" Ki asked.

"Yes. Go on."

She half-smiled and Ki touched her shoulder, smiling in return. They went on.

Endlessly on, through the stony entrails of the earth. The water was higher now, to their knees, and by the time they rounded a sharp bend where the stone walls were polished by ages of water, it had risen to their waists.

"This was a bad idea," Andojar said.

"Maybe," Jessie answered.

"The current," he panted, "it is stronger. Can't you feel it?" He leaned against the wall, breathing slowly. There wasn't much oxygen at this level.

"Quiet!" Ki said sharply. Andojar looked at him with narrowed eyes. Ki gestured for silence.

"What is it, Ki?"

"I hear it too." He looked at Gentle Night, who clung to his arm. "Now I hear it too."

They waded on, and now the sound was nearer. Now they all heard it, but none of them could identify it until they rounded another tight bend in the underground riverbed and suddenly saw the dark, living mass being swept toward them.

Jessie cried out, and she heard Andojar groan with revulsion. They came shrieking and shrilling down the black river, their eyes lighted like hundreds of tiny hot coals by the torchlight.

"Rats!"

Not ten or twenty of them, but rats by the hundreds, swimming or being carried downstream like a fur blanket. They lifted their sharp noses, and the torchlight showed yellow rodent teeth, razor-edged.

They were all around them, and there wasn't a thing to do but stand there and take it. The river swept them past, their shrill voices constant, menacing. Jessie was standing in a current of black and brown rats. They pawed at her as if seeking purchase, a place to climb from the river. They shrilled and their eyes flashed in the light and then they were gone, around a bend in the river, still squeaking and screeching.

"Damn it all," Andojar said. "Damn it all to hell."

"Well," Ki said thoughtfully. "We know now what the cave people could eat besides bats and salamanders."

Andojar made a small, involuntary, disgusted noise. Jessie agreed. Andojar shook his head heavily and they went on again.

"The rats," Ki said, "must have been on the galleon. All those years ago. Rats aren't native to caverns. They came, they bred, they flourished."

"That isn't what puzzles me," Jessie said.

"No? What does?"

"Why were they leaving? Where could they go? What is happening to make them want to go?"

"I hadn't thought of that. Could they sense something?"

"Like what?"

"I don't know," Ki said. "I just don't."

They found the skeletons not far from there. There were fourteen of them, all in a row, lying on a stone ledge two feet above the surface of the water. The torchlight shone on bright metal.

"Gold," Andojar hissed. It was gold. Gold and blackened

133

silver. Each skeleton slept eternally with a bar of gold and a bar of silver beside its disjointed fingers. Each had a sword, rusted, rotted, ruined.

"A burial site. Why the gold?"

"Perhaps they only know that their ancestors worshiped the stuff," Andojar said. "And so they have brought gifts of silver and gold."

"I don't like this," Ki said.

Jessie frowned. "What, Ki? What is it?"

"The burial site. Why would they put their ancestors' bodies here? It wouldn't take much to flood the nook."

"Perhaps they don't care."

"They cared. They wouldn't have carved this alcove, brought the warriors' swords and the gold bars, if they didn't care."

"Then what?"

"The river. It didn't run here before. It is rising. The cavern is flooding."

"What does it mean?" Jessie asked.

"Only the rats know. Something is changing. There are forces at work here, vast forces. Perhaps the cartel's digging has caused things to shift. Perhaps they have diverted the river and have caused . . . I don't know," Ki said. "But I have the feeling. The same feeling the rats had. There is trouble. There is a disaster building. I don't know what it is, or when it will occur, but I don't like it. I don't care for this at all."

They found the galleon next, and all thoughts of imminent disaster were temporarily put aside.

Chapter 13

The river wound away from them, and a stony shelf, a sort of beach, appeared on the right. They clambered up onto it and sat panting, looking at each other in a sort of wonder by the light of the badly faltering torch.

"Well," Andojar said, "perhaps we have gained nothing, but it's a victory to me. I was tired of standing in water."

"I hear it still," Gentle Night said, and she put her hands to her ears, rocking herself back and forth.

"I do too," Jessie said. The voice that cried in pain and fear.

"What do you think?" Jessie said. "A Napai they've captured? Or a cartel worker?"

"Whoever it is, he's in pain," Ki answered.

"Well?"

"Let's see if something can't be done about it," he said, and rose wearily.

"Straight ahead?"

"Yes."

They went on. Suddenly, remarkably, they saw light. Not sunlight, for it was too dim, too smoky for that, but light from a source other than their own torch, and it was so unexpected that Jessie stopped, gripped Andojar's arm, and drew her revolver.

Andojar stood and stared at it. Beyond the elbow in the corridor ahead of them, light played on the walls of stone. They crept on, Ki motioning for silence, frowning as he saw the guns in Jessie's and Andojar's hands. Gentle Night still had the repeating rifle, but she acted as if she had forgotten about it. She followed Ki on with wide eyes, all the ghost stories she had heard as a child, all the tales of the ancients and the haunted mesa coming back vividly to her.

Ki ducked under a low stone lintel, and suddenly he was looking down at it.

It was an incredible sight. Bizarre, unreal, otherworldly. The great galleon, all of her masts snapped off, lay in a stony puddle of stagnant water, canted to one side at an angle of maybe thirty degrees, lighted fiercely by torches, hundreds of torches.

Around her they danced.

They were nearly naked, but many of them had on helmets. Helmets carefully protected from the ravages of time and moisture, bright and shiny helmets. They waved swords as they danced. There was no music, but there was the chanting of voices. The words came to Jessie muffled, indistinct, but the language was clear.

"Spanish," she said with a little gasp.

Andojar and Ki could hear it now, clearly enough to make out that what Jessie had said was true enough. It was Spanish, a mutated form of it, at least. The words were jumbled, the consonants indistinct, the vowels muddy, but it was Spanish.

"Two hundred years," Andojar said in awe. "For two hundred years they have lived here, underground, protecting a ship they do not understand, the metal cargo it carries, the skeletons of their fathers."

136

The cry came again. Easing forward now, Ki could see the captive.

He was an Indian, but not a Napai. Nor a Yuma nor a Papago nor a Cocopa. He wore a feathered headdress and had tattoos on his arms and legs. Around his wrists and ankles were bands of bright metal—gold, most likely. He wore a loincloth and a necklace. He was lying flat on his back, strapped to a wooden bench of some sort, and around him they danced and chanted the garbled words of a language that had no meaning for them other than that it had been spoken by magical creatures—gods—who had come here long ago, and had died.

The Spaniard—another man-thing—came around the corner of the great boulder and saw Ki. His mouth opened, his eyes went wide. Ki tried to reach out and pinch the cluster of nerves at the base of his neck to silence him, but he was too late.

The Spaniard cried out in terror or in anger before Ki's fingertips could find the nerve endings and silence the man. The dancing stopped.

It stopped, and there were only the nearly naked figures standing in the torchlit circle, the great galleon looming behind them, as they stared with haunted eyes toward the ledge where Ki and Jessie stood.

Their leader came forward, crow-hopping, shouting and raising a pointed stick. He led the charge toward the ledge.

Andojar fired from the hip. His first shot hit the leader in the chest. He pitched forward on his face and lay still. The people behind him stopped dead.

"Fire again! Over their heads!" Ki said, and Andojar did. He put three more rounds through the barrel of his Colt .44, and before the echoes had settled to silence, the cavern floor below was empty.

Screaming, crying, the Spaniards ran to the entrances of the many tunnels. They were gone in moments, and there was nothing. Nothing but the firelight and the galleon, the dead Spaniard and the Indian, the ancient one who lay strapped to the wooden table.

They walked toward him, guns in hand, eyes searching the crevices, the tunnel mouths of the great vaulted cavern. The ship, like some ancient monument, seemed to watch them with its many eyes—empty gunports where cannon had bristled once as the great Spanish raider terrorized the native populations of Mexico and Central America, sailing into their harbors to depart laden with gold and silver, religious articles—masks of deities with great ears, fleshy mouths, and knowing eyes. There were cups and goldplate and calendars of gold and silver, circular calendars old beyond European understanding, accurate thousands of years on.

And now she lay empty and gutted, a husk, rotting slowly away in the heart of the honeycombed, ancient mesa thousands of miles from the ports of Spain.

The Indian on the table watched them with stoic eyes as they approached.

"Are you all right?" Andojar asked in Spanish and then in Napai. There was no response. The Indian understood neither language.

"He is," Gentle Night said with certainty, "one of the ancient ones."

"Do you think so? Are they more than a myth?"

"Look at him," Jessie said. "Feathered headdress, gold bracelets. Where have you seen anyone like this? He is from the jungles of the south."

"His culture," Ki said, "is ancient." He untied the Indian. The man lay perfectly still, watching with dark eyes, moving not a muscle until the last knot was undone. Then he slowly rose, and moving with careful dignity, he bowed at Ki's feet and kissed them. Turning to Jessie, he did the same thing.

"No," Andojar said. "Be a man, rise up." But the Indian pledged his loyalty to Andojar and to Gentle Night in the same way.

"They have treated him horribly," Gentle Night said.

She indicated the Indian's chest and abdomen, where hundreds of knife cuts had been incised. Blood still ran freely from many of them, trickling down into the band of his loin cloth.

"They'll do the same to us if they catch us," Andojar pointed out.

"Where are they?"

"Hiding still. For now. They'll get their courage back, I'll bet."

"They're afraid of the guns."

"Maybe. Maybe they're not so scared as we think." Andojar looked around the recesses, the shadowy nooks, the grottoes and tunnels that surrounded them. "They are watching—I feel it."

"I want to see the galleon," Jessie said.

"For God's sake, why!"

"I want to *know*. If all this is for nothing, I want to know it."

"The gold?"

"I want to know if there is a treasure. I want to know if people have been dying for a myth," she said.

"Ki?" Andojar looked the other man in the eye. Perhaps he wanted Ki to tell Jessie not to go to the galleon. Ki just shook his head. Jessica Starbuck was the boss.

They walked to it, the ancient one staying close behind them. A rope ladder, apparently still sound, was tied to the railing of the galleon's deck. Jessie tested it, winked, and started up. The galleon creaked as she stepped onto its splintered, rotten deck. Ki was over the rail and beside her now, and moments later the others.

They started aft, toward the captain's cabin, or what

should have been the captain's cabin.

He was in the cabin. He wore a leather belt with a sword attached, a pair of curled leather boots, a rusted helmet. Everything else had rotted away. The flesh was gone, the heart, the soul. Captain Vasquez had fallen from his chair to lie on the rotted deck. A hollow eye looked up at Jessie.

"He was a very wealthy man," Andojar said distantly.

Ki had moved to the deck. The ship's log lay there, open. It read: ". . . as the good ship rests in this abysmal . . ."

That was all there was. The rest of the page was rotted away. When Ki tried to turn the page, the log crumbled in his hand. What else had been there? A justification, a plea for clemency, a last message to a loved one?

"How do we find the hold?" Jessie asked.

"This way, I think," Ki answered, and they went out and forward to the hatchway. Below it was dark, musty, like a long-dead thing. The ladder was crumbling. The hold smelled of the sea, of slow rot, of time.

Jessie stepped on something and nearly fell. It rolled across the canted deck—another skull. They were everywhere. Bones and skulls and a single rat that had not joined the exodus downstream. The torch flared up brightly as it caught a supply of oxygen from a hatch Ki had kicked open.

The gold shone. It was everywhere—bars and doubloons, Indian masks and utensils, sacred objects, profane objects, shining, gleaming, the wealth of a king, of a whole country carried away to Spain.

"Holy Christ," Andojar said almost reverently.

"How much is here?"

"Millions. Millions," Jessie said. She had never been awed by money, never having been without it, but this was enough to make her shake her head in wonder. Gold by the pound, by the ton, lying deep in the heart of the earth, eternally gleaming, outlasting time and the men who had claimed it.

"It's worth what the cartel is doing."

"They can't know it's here—not for sure."

"No."

"Can we get it out, Ki?"

He shook his head. "There isn't any way. They'll find it, and they'll be richer yet. And the rest of the world a little poorer—the money will buy still more power for them."

The ancient one had been standing silently beside them. Now, as they watched, he fell to his knees again. He pointed at a gold mask and then at his own face, tracing the large ears, the Oriental eyes.

"What does he want?"

"To take it, I think. Maybe he knows what it is. His people came from the far south too."

Jessie nodded, and when the Indian hesitated still, she bent down and handed him the mask, which seemed to be some sort of religious relic. The Indian kissed her feet again, and Jessie could only stand in embarrassment and allow it.

"Now what?"

"Now we get the hell out of here."

"Easier said than done."

"We have a guide," Ki pointed out.

They looked to the ancient one. "Him?"

"He got in here. He has to know the way. His people have lived here a long while."

"All right. I'll believe it. How do we make him understand that we—"

The first tremor came then. They felt the ship move slightly underfoot, as if it were under way on a gentle sea. Then there was a trickling of stone and dust, like rain on the deck above them. Ki looked at Jessie.

"The rats."

141

"What about them?"

"I think they had good reason for leaving."

Andojar was worried. "Do you mean what I think you mean?"

"I mean the mesa is rotten. I think the rats sensed an earth movement."

"That one?" Andojar asked.

"No. Not that one. This one will be larger, much larger. Enough to take the mesa down."

"You can't mean it!"

"I mean it. I fear it. Talk to the ancient one. He must be made to understand—we have to get out of here. I believe this. We must leave or die here. Leave or remain behind as permanently as Captain Vasquez and his men."

It took a lot of pointing and gesturing, but finally light dawned in the priest's eyes. He nodded vigorously and pointed upward.

"The others—if there are others—may not like him bringing us out."

"No. They're shy of strangers. But I don't think they're a violent people. Remember the one who befriended the Napai, Nakipa?"

"Are we going to debate it?" Jessie asked. "You know there's no choice. If there is a way out, only the ancient one knows it. We trust him to lead us out, or we die."

The second tremor came then. It lasted a little longer. The deck groaned as the gold shifted. A large rock fell from the cavern ceiling and struck the deck above them.

"Let's go. Now," Ki said. No one argued.

They started out, Ki leading the way. He started down the rope ladder, the priest carrying the gold mask behind him, Jessie next.

As Ki's foot touched down, he heard the whisper of bare feet against stone behind him, and crouching, he turned.

The sword in the Spaniard's hand sang past his head. If he hadn't ducked instinctively, his own decapitated skull would have joined the others hidden in the cavern.

Ki ducked, came up with stiffened fingers, and struck at the Spaniard's larynx. The fingertips struck cartilage and the attacker fell back strangling, clutching his throat. Ki turned gracefully, lifting his leg for a kick as he pivoted.

The second attacking Spaniard caught a crushing blow on the temple and went down in a heap. There was a third man to Ki's right, and a *tobi-geri*, or flying kick, took him down as Ki's foot struck the man's chest above the heart.

Jessie clung helplessly to the ladder, unable to go up or down, to draw her gun, and the Spaniard with the pointed stick must have thought she was going to be easy prey. He moved in, crow-hopping, wanting to impale her. He never saw the shiny *shuriken* whir toward him, tearing into his throat. He went down with a cry of agony, blood spraying everywhere from a severed carotid artery.

There were others out there, hidden in the shadows, but they held back now, mesmerized by this fighting machine, this man who must have seemed superhuman. Andojar fired two shots as well, and remembering clearly what those guns could do, the descendants of the Spanish renegades ran away once more.

Jessie and Andojar joined Ki on the ground. Gentle Night followed. It was she who pointed it out.

"The water—look. It rises."

It *was* rising. The galleon had lifted slightly. The water around their feet was six inches deeper. The earth moved again and this time a stone column toppled, spilling rock across the floor of the cavern. The tremor lasted a good five minutes. There was nothing at all to do except stand braced and wait for it to pass, to stand and look up at the ceiling of stone above them and hope.

"Come on," Ki said, for the ancient one had started on, still clutching his golden mask. They followed after him, hurrying on into the unknown. Behind them, shadowy figures moved in the cavern, their voices rising in an angry murmur. There was another tremor, and then another, and the rock began to fall.

Chapter 14

The ancient one led them through a maze of tunnels. The tremors came one after another now, and rock fell from the ceilings like deadly rain. They found one tunnel blocked by stone and had to detour.

"What if there's no way out left?" Jessie asked. "The passages could all be blocked."

"Hurry," was all Ki could say. And they had to hurry. The ancient one was spry and quick despite his wounds, and he scuttled through the maze of the cavern, his gold mask clutched to his chest, his eyes bright, searching the passages for the way out.

Up. It was up they had to go, for that was the way the priest was taking. Upward, toward the mesa top. To the home of the ancient ones. It became hard to breathe. The oxygen was low. Stone dust filled the air at times. They were climbing rapidly now, following a narrow trail that rubbed Jessie's shoulders on either side. Upward—and the ceiling lowered, the tunnel became steeper, the floor of it rougher, more littered with fresh debris.

"Ki!" Jessie yelled, and he just had time to spring to one side. Rock fell from the ceiling in a cataract of stone. Boulders careened away down the long tunnel. Ki stood and dusted his hands together, his breathing a little ragged.

They climbed slowly, steadily, winding, twisting, taking small side tunnels, detouring.

"We'd never find our way back if he wanted to leave us," Jessie noted. She paused for breath. "Let alone find our way out," she continued.

"The man's gratitude was sincere," Ki replied.

"At the time. He's had an hour to think over the impulse."

But the ancient one seemed to have nothing on his mind except getting out of the cavern, and quickly.

They came suddenly to a huge vaulted alcove. Below, stalagmites stood in profusion, many-colored, red and wavering in the firelight. The ancient one looked them over, and then he sat down to rest.

"At last."

"Well, we know he's human," Jessie said. Gentle Night was still standing.

"What is it?"

"There is someone back there."

"The Spaniards, but they won't—"

"Someone else. I can hear hard shoes. Leather shoes on stone."

"It's not possible," Andojar said.

"Why not?" Jessie asked. "We don't even know where we are. If the cartel broke through into the tunnels, they could be anywhere."

"Searching for us?"

"For the gold. If they find us, well and good. If they find us accidentally, the results will be the same as if they searched on purpose."

"I hope they do come," Andojar said. But he was still grieving for his father, and they paid him no mind. The ancient one was already on his feet again, looking with puzzlement, perhaps with despair, back down the tunnels in the direction Gentle Night believed the *bandidos* were coming from.

He inclined his head and formed a soundless word with his lips.

"He's ready to go," Ki said, rising.

"Poor bastard," Andojar said. "They keep invading his world, don't they? First down in the jungles, then here. The Spaniards came. Then us. Now the cartel and Santana's people. Now they have come and they've started digging at the mesa until the whole damn thing is ready to fall apart, until his world is ready to collapse finally."

They went on, the torch flickering low, the corridor of stone they followed away from the great alcove slanting upward slightly, widening.

They came around the elbow in the trail and came face to face with Santana's men.

It was hard to tell who was more surprised. Santana himself wasn't there, but half a dozen of his men were. The redhead, Gore, was among them.

He reached for his gun and Jessie shot him through the forearm. Gore howled with pain and fell back, sitting down on the corridor's floor. The *bandidos* had had a dozen Indian slaves with them, men carrying shovels and picks, and at the first shot they took off at a dead run.

A slim Comanchero to Gore's left reached for his Peacemaker, but he was a shade slower than Andojar, who brought his big ivory-gripped .44s up and fired with either hand, nonchalantly but with deadly efficiency.

The Comanchero was blown away, paying for the rapes and murders of the last five years with his own hot blood.

The Apache was the dangerous one. He had a face like chipped stone, and a knife the length of his arm. He swung out with it and Andojar screamed with pain. Jessie shot the

147

Apache in the face and they withdrew as the *bandidos* broke and ran.

"My arm . . ." Andojar groaned.

"You're all right."

"Sure." Blood was flowing unchecked from the gash across his forearm. Bone showed through the layers of flesh. Jessie tried to bandage it with her scarf. It wasn't doing much to stop the blood. "My right-hand gun," Andojar said through a grimace of pain, "I dropped it."

"Forget it."

"I want it."

Ki repeated, "Forget it." They were still withdrawing. The *bandidos* hadn't come on yet, but they would, their Prussian masters would see to it. Ki and Jessie backed away, carrying Andojar's weight.

And behind them were the Spaniards.

The tremor nearly knocked Ki from his feet. Rock fell in a trickle from above. The ground shook and rolled. Dust sifted through the air, choking them.

"How is he?" Ki asked. Andojar's cry of pain answered the question. The Napai wasn't the sort to cry out easily. He had the blood of conquistadores, the blood of Indians in him. He had lived hard and he had lived bravely. He wasn't one to give in to pain unless it was so intense that his body, acting on its own, cried out for help, for relief from the hurting.

There was a shout from ahead of them, a shout of joy, a savage thing. The Spaniards were coming. The man-things. Ki looked around anxiously.

"There!" It was Gentle Night who called out. The ancient one had found a way out of the trap. A tunnel exiting straight up from the corridor.

"Is he sure?" Jessie asked.

"How can we ask him?"

148

From behind, shots rang out, and again they were trapped in a tunnel with deadly ricochets. Ahead of them the man-things began their chanting.

"We'd better trust him. It's the only way."

The ancient one, somehow managing to hold his gold mask, was already up and through the attic-like opening. Ki followed, reaching back to help Jessie hoist Andojar. Gentle Night followed, with Jessie coming last.

"Quiet," Ki hissed. "There is a chance they won't find us."

Andojar began to moan again, and Jessie smothered his mouth with her lips.

Below the chanting grew louder and they came—the man-things, the Spaniards, the cave-dwellers, a hundred of them, men and half-naked, dirty women carrying ancient sabers and pointed, fire-hardened sticks.

Ki saw their heads, their matted dark hair, the skins and ancient leather garments they dressed in.

Santana's people came from the opposite direction, guns at the ready, and when they saw the Spaniards they opened fire, their guns roaring, filling the cavern depths as the Spaniards, still chanting, marched forward or flew toward the enemy, hurling themselves on the *bandidos,* driving their sticks into hearts and lungs and eyes and bowels until it looked like a mad scene out of hell, an inferno where the dying writhed on the stony floor while smoke and flame rolled through the honeycombed mesa.

Screams of pain and the angry, challenging shouts of warriors entering battle rang in their ears. It went on for minutes, for hours, until finally it settled to a sighing, muf-fled weeping, to sobs and death rattles. Ki didn't even look below to see what had happened. He had no wish to look upon Armageddon.

"Come," Ki said. "We must go."

He lifted Jessie to her feet. The priest lay atop his gold mask, protecting it with his own body. Ki spoke gently to him. "The battle is over. Let's go."

Again a tremor came, and this time Ki was knocked to the ground. They lay gripping the stone beneath them—the insubstantial, shifting stone—and waited, waited the eternity until it passed.

"All right," Ki said, "we go."

"Ki." Jessie touched his arm. "If we do make it out—to the top of the mesa—it's not going to do us a lot of good, is it? If the mesa goes—well, then we're all dead no matter what we do. It won't matter if we're inside the caves or on top of the mountain. When it goes, we're done for."

Ki didn't answer. What was there to say? Hoisting Andojar to his feet, they started on once more.

The torch flickered and hesitated and then went out.

"Strike a match," Andojar said through his pain.

Ki tried it. The torch wouldn't take. There was a moment's light, blue and yellow, from the match, and then darkness descended again.

They stood there in the blackness, feeling despair begin to become a real presence. "What now?" Jessie asked. The Indian touched her shoulder and she recoiled reflexively before she realized he meant no harm.

She told Ki, "He's taking my hand."

"Very romantic," Andojar said. In his delirium it seemed amusing to him and he laughed. No one else did.

"He wants us to lead us out," Ki said.

"In the darkness!" Gentle Night couldn't believe that it was possible.

"He's lived near here all his life."

"No one could know these caverns by touch."

"We'll see. There's not much choice."

Linking hands, they started on. Jesse fell and knocked

her chin. Ki and the Indian helped her up. Ki led Andojar, who was faltering badly. Gentle Night held the former *bandido*'s other hand.

And they followed the priest on. The blind leading the blind. Upward still, while around them the earth rumbled. Far below, voices crying out in pain, in anger, in fear sounded from the depths of the cavern.

"What was that?" Jessie asked.

"What?"

"A breeze. Something touched my cheek."

"There's a wind of sorts in these caverns. We've already discovered that."

"This was different," she insisted. "Somehow different."

They trudged on, stumbling, falling, the darkness surrounding them with anxiety. Now and then the tremors came, twice hard enough to knock them down and set the stone in the ceiling to falling.

"There!" Jessie cried out, and Ki felt her yank her hand from his to point upward, to point at the small shining point of promise, at the light.

"I don't see it," Gentle Night said, and then she did. "Oh yes, there! Was anything ever so beautiful?"

Andojar let out a sigh of relief. They were nearly out, it was nearly over, the endless darkness, the endless roaming in the tunnels. They staggered the last few yards and stood beneath a hole in the ceiling, one that time and water had bored in the caprock. They stood and looked up at the blue sky.

Indians with war axes in their hands looked back.

"Who are they?"

"Ancient ones. Look at their feathered headdresses, the plumes, the gold ornaments."

"They look real happy to see us, don't they?" Jessie said softly. In fact, they looked ready to kill. They had been discovered in their secret world and they didn't like it a bit.

The priest held up the gold mask. He spoke rapidly in an ancient tongue to those who stood above. Their eyes were dull and menacing, their faces openly hostile. The priest's words didn't seem to be softening them up much.

"Trouble," Andojar said. "They want to kill us."

Most of the arguing was being done by the priest and a young chief with scars all over his arms and face. Self-inflicted scars, it seemed. Some sort of religious mortification, Jessie guessed.

Maybe Andojar was wrong, but it seemed he was correct. The young chief wanted them dead, these intruders. They could read it in his eyes, even if they couldn't understand the words. *Death*. When the Indians finally lowered a rope ladder and Jessie shinnied up, she saw the man face to face, and the eyes carried the same dreadful message.

Death.

The priest argued all the way up the ladder, and then he stood with the gold mask high in the air, showing it to all the people, all of these ancient ones who had gathered on top of the wind-swept mesa at sundown to see these strangers from below, from out of the heart of Mesa Grande, with the odd languages and odd-colored skins and eyes, with the strange dress. They stood and watched as the priest held the gold mask overhead and the reddish glow of sunset burnished it with bright, fiery hues.

And they didn't look convinced at all.

The two priests argued furiously for a time, and then suddenly all conversation stopped. A boy of fourteen was dispatched toward the rocks beyond a screen of sagebrush. Everyone waited in silence while sundown painted the vast land and stained the empty sky. The breeze flowed across them, cooling and fresh, carrying the scents of a free outside world.

When the youth came back, he had the old one with him.

The man had a seamed, wrinkled face. He hobbled along on a knobby cane. He had white hair down to his waist. He approached slowly, as if eternity were only a breath away, of no importance.

He spoke to Gentle Night, and Andojar's head came up sharply. He whispered, "Napai. He speaks Napai, this old one. Says he used to sneak away from the camp. He had a friend who was Napai. Long ago. Fifty years. He knows the tongue still."

Gentle Night translated most of it. The first words were ominous. She turned to Ki and Jessie and told them quietly, "The old man says we must die. We have made the earth tremble. We have brought death. It is our duty to give our living hearts on the stone so that the mesa may be appeased."

"To *what?*" Ki asked. "Give our hearts to *what*, Gentle Night?"

"It is their custom. Something brought with them from the jungles where the red and green birds live, and the little furry men swing in the trees. They have a stone and it drinks blood. The young chief, the priest, he wishes to take our hearts and pacify the spirits with them, with our blood and flesh."

"What does the other one tell them? The priest with the mask."

Gentle Night hesitated, listening before she nodded and asked her question of the old man.

"He says that you are good people. You have saved his life. You have recovered an ancient relic, one he had long searched for. It seems the people would rather have our hearts than the mask."

Jessie stepped forward and put a hand on Gentle Night's shoulder. "You tell them this—this mountain is ready to cave in. It's old and rotten and if we don't get off it we're all going to die, and no number of hearts sacrificed to the spirits is going to stop it."

As if to punctuate her speech, a new tremor went through the mesa, rippling and grumbling beneath them. Gentle Night translated Jessie's words.

The old man spoke to both leaders and then to several other men who stepped forward to have their say. It took a long time for them to decide.

"They are going to wait," Andojar told them.

Gentle Night explained more fully. "They are going to keep us prisoner until the oracle can be consulted."

"What oracle?"

"I don't know. I couldn't understand that part."

"The young priest doesn't like it," Jessie said. "He has his knife all whetted and ready, I guess."

He was glowering. He turned his head as Jessie looked at him, and spat. "Well-mannered, too."

"Jessie," Andojar said, "we can't wait here while they look at the entrails of a badger or count the stars through the hole in the roof or throw sticks to decide what to do. This mountain's coming down! Everyone in it, on it, is going to die."

"We can't do much about it. We can't fight and we can't run."

"I can fight," the wounded gunman said.

Maybe. Maybe he could have done the job with just his left-hand gun, but he never got the chance to try. As if the ancient ones had understood Andojar or could read his mind, they surged forward and arms were thrown around them, rawhide ties produced, their bodies searched for knives, their guns taken, and as sunset purpled the mesa top, shadowing the broad desert beyond, they were hustled off toward the city of the ancient ones, toward their prison cell.

★

Chapter 15

It was of stone, that was what surprised Jessie most. The city of the ancients, low and solidly built on top of Mesa Grande, was made of stone. Twice Jessie saw miniature pyramids, steps leading up their flanks. They were built very small, very low, as was everything on the mesa, to keep curious eyes from easily detecting the city.

They were led through a street paved with stones, and women in bark skirts, children with Oriental eyes stared at them. At the end of the street was a large building square, with a complicated courtyard like a stone maze.

They were led through that as dusk settled. From narrow windows, more men in feathered bonnets stared out. In the center of the courtyard, the exact center, lay a flat stone. It was eight feet by ten, weather-pocked. Blood grooves had been cut along the edges. In the middle of the stone was a sun design, stained darkly.

Beyond that was another low stone wall and then the building where they were led to be locked away until the priests decided whether it was to be life or death. In all probability, Jessie thought, they would meet their deaths there as a last earth tremor leveled the mesa.

The door was of stone, and it fitted so well that there wasn't even a whisper of sound as it was shut behind them. They stood there in the darkness, isolated again, enclosed again. Jessie had a sudden pang of desire for the wide Texas plains, for the great Circle Star Ranch, where you could ride all day and never see another soul, and if you rode in the right direction you'd never see anything at all higher than a prairie dog's shoulder.

She walked to where Andojar had sagged against the wall. "How are you doing, *bandido?*"

"Well enough. Are you sorry you came out here, Jessie? Sorry that you took pity on a poor band of dirty Indians?"

"No. Not that we've helped them much. But I met you, so it's been fine." She stroked Andojar's dark hair and kissed him on the forehead. "I'm not sorry, nor is Ki. Are you, Ki?"

Ki didn't answer. He was distracted. Standing in the middle of the stone cell, he was looking upward toward the ceiling fifteen feet above. Beyond that was a square stone chimney or air vent, and beyond that he could see a single star flickering against the smoky darkness of the twilight sky.

"They left an opening here."

"They left it because no one can get out that way," Andojar said. He winced and bit off a cry of pain as Jessie removed her bloody scarf from his wounded right arm. Dried blood stuck to cloth, and as it tore free, fresh blood began to flow again.

"We need clean cloth."

"And a surgeon," Andojar said. Jessie smiled faintly and began to bandage the wound again, using the sleeve of her blouse. Ki continued to gaze upward.

"Forget it, Ki," Andojar said. "It can't be done."

"Perhaps not." Still Ki looked. The stone vent was three feet on a side, maybe rising twenty feet. To reach it was a jump of fifteen feet. Of course, he could get help there. The climb on that apparently seamless stone would be difficult, but . . .

"Impossible," Andojar repeated.

"I don't think so. What else can we do? Wait until they come for us? Until the oracle has decreed death, that our living hearts be cut out?"

"Ki," Jessie said, "even if you could make it, I know I can't. Andojar can't."

"One outside might make the difference," Gentle Night said. "Perhaps we can make a rope."

"Where does the vent lead? Straight up," Andojar pointed out. "You'll be invisible."

The earthquake, when it came that time, was like a rumbling explosion. Ki was slammed against the wall and a great square stone fell from the ceiling. Down the street, someone cried in fear. They could hear chanting again, always chanting, as if they were near a temple.

"I'm going to go," Ki said after the tremor had passed. "There will be no one alive on this mesa tomorrow."

"He's right," Jessie agreed. To Ki she said, "Don't fall, Ki. Things wouldn't be much good without you."

Her hand lingered for a moment on his shoulder and then fell away. He looked at her with veiled emotion for a minute, then turned and said to the women, "A boost up. If you can carry my weight, let me stand on your shoulders."

"You still won't be high enough. Fifteen feet to the mouth of the shaft."

"Then I'll fly," Ki said with a lightness he didn't feel. His eyes went to the stone that had fallen. "That! Can we roll it over here?"

They couldn't roll it, but with all of them working they

157

managed to slide it slowly toward the area below the vent. The women climbed up on it and linked arms. Then Ki, as lightly as an acrobat, lifted himself onto their shoulders and sprang upward.

He had seen a small niche, a slight handhold, and now his fingers caught it. One foot went up and he used it to brace himself as his free hand went behind him to the opposite wall. Now, with his legs in front of him, his back pressed to the wall behind him, he began to inch his way upward, using the tension of his leg muscles to hold him in place.

It was slow business. He could see Gentle Night and Jessie below him, looking up as he crept toward the single beckoning star above him.

Sweat broke from his forehead. The air down the ventilating shaft seemed cold and harsh. His muscles ached as he moved upward an inch at a time, pressing his legs against the wall until they burned and throbbed with the effort. The mouth of the shaft seemed a hundred feet, a hundred years away. And when he reached it, what then? They would very likely see him, and that would be that—it would be only so much wasted effort.

Ki looked up and realized with a start that he was nearly there. All he had to do was stretch out a hand, grab the rim of the shaft, and haul himself up and over.

He was there, balanced like a man atop a chimney, looking down at the rooftops, at the courtyard below, where something was occurring. The oracle, Ki decided, had demanded death. Men in strange costumes, in wooden masks, stood near a fire that had been built atop the sacrificial stone. Ki wiped at his eyes and peered downward in the other direction. Rooftops, empty windows, some sort of grain-storage bin.

None of that was of any help. He would have to go

straight down, try to overpower the guards at the front door and lead the others through the stone maze. There were hundreds of ancient ones out there waiting to stop them. Still, he thought, you tried. You always kept trying. Stop and you know you are dead.

Ki climbed down the shaft. It was roughly fitted outside, offering many foot- and handholds. He was to the roof quickly, looking over the edge at the heads of two guards who stood in the manner of all guards, half alert, half bored, looking toward the fire across the courtyard where the excitement was. They carried spears with iron heads—which did them no good at all.

Ki turned, hung suspended for a moment, and dropped to the ground. A hand-heel blow to the chin disabled the man to his right. An elbow rising into the face of the guard on the left smashed his nose and dropped him to the stone.

Ki moved to the stone door, found the iron mechanism that unlocked it, and swung it inward.

"Come on," he hissed.

"Ki!" Gentle Night cried out.

"Quickly," he said urgently, "and quietly."

It was already too late for silence. Before they had gotten Andojar to the door they could hear the sound of rushing footsteps, and as they stepped into the courtyard they saw them coming, fifty or sixty ancient ones armed with lances, their hearts filled with only one thought—kill the outsiders, appease the spirit of the mountain.

Ki grabbed Jessie's arm and yanked her to the side, racing with her down the stone alley that the maze formed. Looking back over his shoulder to see that Gentle Night and Andojar were with them, he sped on.

They came to a tall stone wall. There were voices on the far side, voices and torchlight—and the voices were speaking Spanish.

"The Spaniards," Ki whispered. He crouched beside the wall, Jessie with him. Andojar and Gentle Night came quietly up beside them. The night, seemingly ready to erupt with sound and violence, was dead silent for a long minute.

Then the storm broke. They heard the voices rising shrilly as the Spaniards, gushing up out of the cavern below, attacked the city of the ancients. Some sort of outbuilding was afire, and already the death cries were in the air.

"Now," Ki said. "Let's go."

"Where?"

"Off the mesa, out of here. It's a war zone and it's going to get worse."

Ki led them away from the stone courtyard, weaving through the maze. From above, he had seen how it ran, and there was no problem there. What was a problem was the pair of ancient ones they met in the narrow passage.

The first yelled and threw his iron-headed spear at Ki, who crouched and caught the shaft of the spear with his forearm, slapping it away as he ducked to one side. The second, seeing that, decided to thrust rather than throw. He came in at Ki, his spear held low, and dug up toward the belly. Ki's crossed forearms blocked the spear, his hands closed around its shaft. Jerking upward, he ripped the spear from the Indian's hands and kicked out simultaneously, planting his toes in the man's testicles. The ancient one fell back with a cry of pain.

"Hurry!" Andojar said.

There was no need for the reminder. They were caught between two inimical armies. There was fire in the skies, and sounds of battle rose on the wind.

They started at a run down the stone-paved streets of the city of the ancients. From the end of the street a ragged army appeared, skin-clad, their hair matted and tangled. There were women in this army, looking as battle-tough and as filthy as the men with their pointed-stick weapons, their swords. Two or three wore helmets, rusted, eroded.

Ki pulled Jessie into an alleyway and the four of them crouched there, waiting for the half-human army to pass.

The tremors began again. The first one hit like a bolt of lightning with following thunder. The building next to Ki sagged, groaned, and collapsed.

"For God's sake," Andojar said, "it's coming down! The whole goddamn mesa's coming down!"

"Let's go, now!" Ki said. The wall on the far side of the street came down now with a crash. A woman, naked and confused, fell with the pile of stone and was crushed to death. Behind them the battle raged, and not even the anger of the Mesa Grande spirits could stop the killing as the "conquistadores," like an invading army risen from a mass grave, swept through the city of the ancient ones.

There was much fire. Despite appearances, there had to have been a lot of wood behind the stone walls of the city. Flame stretched skyward, lighting a miniature pyramid. Jessie paused to watch through the smoke and flame as the pyramid collapsed and a cloud of dust spun upward, obscuring the stars.

Andojar touched her shoulder and she turned, running with the others toward the darkness beyond the city.

In front of them the earth suddenly opened, and a fissure half a mile deep yawned up at them.

"This way," Jessie said, turning away toward the east, dragging Andojar, who was weak and perhaps slightly confused from lack of blood, after her.

They were into the sagebrush now, the chaparral and manzanita. It grew to head height and higher. There was no visible trail, only the darkness. Underfoot there was a rumbling like a muffled detonation, distant thunder, or mine work.

No one spoke. They ran on, their lungs afire, legs heavy, eyes searching for the rim of the mesa, which had to be there somewhere ahead of them.

"We'll never make it down if we do find the edge."

"We'll damn sure try."

Andojar went down. He just didn't have it left in him. Ki and Jessie hoisted him to his feet and they started on again.

"The pool," he muttered.

"What? I can't hear you." Jessie stumbled herself, caught her balance, and waited for Andojar's panting reply.

"The pool. The hidden canyon. I know the way up from there."

"You've been up here from the canyon?" Ki asked.

"Sure. Halfway, at least." He could barely hold his head up now. "Where are we? Not a hard climb if we can find the canyon."

"Gentle Night?"

She looked to the stars and said, "We are going right. Eastward. We need to be on the east rim. The canyon . . . there!" She had spotted a landmark peak across the desert, a dark, bulky hill like a beacon of hope.

"Which way?"

"Onward. I don't know. Hurry!"

Again the ground shook and they could feel the mesa move underneath them—the whole rotten, improbable, time-locked mesa.

Ki nearly ran off into space. He broke from the mat of sage and chia, of greasewood and scrub juniper, and nearly stepped off into the emptiness below.

Gentle Night grabbed him and yanked him back. It was half a mile straight down. Ki looked down and then back across the flat mesa to the burning city.

"The canyon," Andojar said weakly.

"Gentle Night?"

"I don't see it. I can't see a thing. Wait. The mission!" She pointed. "There. And there is the village. Not far then, not far."

"Where, Andojar? Which way down?"

Andojar was beyond talking. The loss of blood had caught up with him, the long run through the night, the fighting, the days without food. He lifted his head but could say nothing cogent.

Ki hefted the man across his shoulders and they started on, eyes searching the darkness, looking for a way down, knowing that to fail in finding it was to die.

"There!" Gentle Night grabbed Jessie's arm and pointed down. Below, the pool in the hidden canyon, the pool where Jessie and Andojar had made love, glinted dully in the starlight.

"Can you see a way down?"

"There. Maybe. Jesus, if Andojar thought this was an easy climb..."

"He only came halfway up, remember, Jessie?"

Ki looked over the edge of the mesa himself, seeing only sheer slope, an eyebrow of a trail that the ancients might have used to fetch water from the pool in times of drought. If so, he thought, they had great balance, these survivors of another time.

"What do we do?"

"Try it."

"You can't do it carrying Andojar," Jessie said.

"We can't leave him. We'll try," Ki answered.

That was all a man could do.

Gentle Night went first. The Napai girl was quick and sure as she half-climbed, half-skidded to the head of the winding, narrow trail. The rumbling from within the mesa sounded again and it summoned answering thunder from above, from the sky to the north.

"Christ," Jessie breathed. "Shot through with luck."

There was a storm building, a rapid summer storm that could sweep across the desert and dump buckets of water down over them, creating flash floods. Lightning struck distantly. Jessie, following Gentle Night, hurried on, wondering if they hadn't in fact offended some ancient gods. The elements seemed to be lashing out angrily, Nature using all of her weapons to sweep the living from the desert.

The wind began to roar and howl. Nothing was secure. Nothing was safe. The earth moved, rock fell, the wind slapped at them. Jessie looked back to see Ki, his hair lifted by the rising wind, his face illuminated by distant lightning, carrying Andojar down the long, narrow trail. Below was the canyon where the ancients had carved their maps, their symbols. Below was the long canyon where flash floods had swept house-sized boulders down as other angry storms had assaulted the desert.

The rain began. A few drops at first, incredibly large. Jessie's cheek was stung by a single raindrop, and in moments, as the skies opened up, she was soaked clear through. Her clothes hung heavily on her. It was impossible to see except when the lightning struck.

The trail was there and then it wasn't, as a tremor or a freshet or both swept a part of it away from underfoot and Jessie fell off into space. She clawed at the earth and found a tentative grip. She cried out for help, but no one saw her, no one could have heard her. For a moment it seemed she was going to fall the rest of the way to the valley floor, now five hundred feet below them, but at the last moment her sliding, desperate hand found a stony outcrop and she managed to grip it with her torn and bleeding fingers and drag herself up onto the trail once more.

It rained fiercely for an hour. The trail grew wider and

less steep, and rounding a last bend in the trail, Jessie suddenly found herself standing on flat ground, in the heart of the deep canyon, the mesa towering over them.

"Ki?"

"I'm here, Jessie."

"And Gentle Night?"

"Beside me. We have Andojar. Where are you?"

She walked through the darkness and rain until she found them once more. Before them the river, born only minutes ago, destined to die before the hour was done, rushed by— a white, frothing, violent thing.

"Well," Jessie said, "we can't cross that. Which way?"

"Any way. We just have to get away from the mesa. It's due. Overdue. It's a dying thing and we're beneath it."

They started down the canyon then, the river on their left. Ahead lay the Napai village, the mission. And Santana, who was waiting at the head of the canyon.

Chapter 16

He was lean and dark and feral. The dark slicker he wore glistened dully. The Colt in his hand was big and blue-black. Behind him stood half a dozen other men.

"Is that him?" Santana asked.

"Who?"

"Him, damn you—is that Andojar!" Reaching out, he grabbed a handful of hair and yanked Andojar's head up, then slowly he smiled. "Bastard," he muttered, and his gunsight raked a deep groove across Andojar's face. Ki, holding the man over his shoulders, could do little that wasn't suicidal.

"Leave him alone!" Gentle Night threw herself at the *bandido* and was knocked flat. Jessie already had burly arms around her. Burly, dirty arms. The man had the breath of a coyote.

"What do you want?" Ki asked.

"Him. I want to kill him."

"Why?"

"Why?" Santana seemed genuinely surprised. "He left us. He brought me here, he taught me to be what I am, and then he left."

"He got smart."

"He became a coward. It was having priest's blood in him that did it. I know," Santana said.

"What are you going to do with us?"

"I would kill you too. Now." He nodded his head in the opposite direction. "But *they* want you."

"They?"

"The Europeans. The men in the dark suits."

"The Prussians?"

Santana shrugged. "If you say so." It was of no importance to him. Only revenge was important. He meant to take revenge now on Andojar.

One of his lieutenants spoke up. "The river, Santana. If we don't hurry, we won't get out of here either."

It was a fact. The river, swollen by the thunderstorm, rushed and ranted down the narrow gorge, white against the darkness of night. Santana looked at it uncertainly.

"They won't like it if we don't bring the prisoners to them tonight."

"What do I care about them?" Santana snarled, but obviously he did care. The cartel was paying him very well— and the work, which merely involved terrorizing a bunch of ragged Indians, was much easier than, say, robbing a bank or a payroll shipment.

He looked at Andojar, lifted one side of his mouth in a crooked sneer, and said, "All right—we go. Leave the pretty woman alone. She's mine. I always liked yellow-haired women."

Ki's guts were boiling with fury, but he held himself back. They were started down the canyon, walking a narrow trail beside the wild river.

Gentle Night was there and then she was gone.

She leaped for the river, and before anyone could do more than call out, she was gone, bobbing away, a mo-

168

mentary dark stain against the frothing river.

"Keep hold of the others. Don't let them try it."

"She'll drown, Santana."

"What do I care?" the *bandido* asked. "What do I care about some stinking Indian woman?"

"The water's still rising," his nervous lieutenant said.

"I got eyes! All right. Keep hold of the others. Where are those damned horses?"

"I can see them. In the brush."

"Where are we going?" Jessie asked.

"I told you, didn't I? To see these foreigners that want you, Miss Starbuck."

"But where are they?"

"None of your damn business, but I'll tell you—at the new tunnel."

"Inside the mesa?" Jessie couldn't believe it. Didn't they realize that the mountain was ready to cave in?

"That's right. We been blasting over there. Where were you that you didn't hear it?" Santana peered at Jessie, his thoughts unreadable.

"We were inside."

"Yeah? Well, then, you heard the blasting."

"We *felt* it." Jessie looked helplessly at Ki. Was there any point in trying to tell Santana anything? He was a man with a one-track mind, an obedient if murderous lackey. But the cartel men—they couldn't be so stupid. Maybe they had no choice, however; maybe to fail the cartel would mean death for them. Failure was the same as suicide.

Ki was thinking along the same lines, but he was distracted by thoughts of Gentle Night. Could she have survived that plunge into the raging river? If she had, she was certainly better off than she would have been with the *bandidos,* but it seemed uncharacteristic of her to escape on her own.

"It was for the best," Ki said under his breath. "At least one of us got out."

As for the three remaining, it seemed very doubtful indeed. Andojar could barely walk. Ki and Jessie were bound, guarded by armed men. And once the cartel men had Jessie under their eyes, they wouldn't dare let her escape.

They found the horses concealed in the heavy brush, and Ki was swung up to sit in the wet saddle, Jessie on a horse beside him. Andojar was thrown over the back of another horse, and Santana himself led them out of the brushy feeder canyon, back toward the flats where pools of water gleamed in the starlight, steel-gray and still. In twenty-four hours they would be gone, soaked up by the thirsty sands.

They rode silently. Once Ki felt Jessie's eyes on him and he glanced that way, shaking his head. There wasn't much to be done about things. He still had a few *shuriken* concealed in his vest pockets, but he couldn't get at them with his hands bound, nor would they be much good against a dozen guns.

They rode in silence across the damp, cool desert as the moon began its slow ascent, a thin, curved moon like a secret eye slowly opening.

Jessie formulated a dozen plans and discarded them all. There wasn't any way out at all, there just wasn't. Her horse stumbled and she yanked back hard on the reins to keep its head up.

It wasn't until they were past it that she realized what had caused the misstep. There was a narrow, snaking fissure winding its way across the desert floor. Now she saw another and another, like strands of a web raying out from the mesa, which was at its center.

The explosion flashed a yellow ball of light against the sky. They were blasting, as Santana had said.

"They'll blow that mountain down!"

170

"I guess they know what they're doing," Santana said. "We been blasting all day."

"It's rotten clear through. It can't stand anything like that!"

"Hell, it's a mountain, ain't it?" Santana smiled crookedly. "If you don't like it, you tell them, okay?"

"Someone has gotten anxious," Ki said. "Work was going too slowly for the cartel."

"They'll never make it. The mesa's bound to come down."

"Like the man says, tell *them*."

They rode on. Now they could see the mouth of the new tunnel, which was slightly to the south of the old. Indian slaves worked frantically, clearing away rubble. Torchlight flickered on the desert floor. Dust still hung heavy in the air from the blast.

They dismounted just as thunder sounded again in the north and lightning sparked. They were rushed inside, Jessie shoved by Santana, Ki led by a rope tied to his wrists, Andojar carried between two men.

There was a beehive of activity inside the new shaft, laborers, overseers, carts, and mules moving in different directions.

The two men in dark suits turned slowly at Santana's approach. One was thickset and blond, the other tall and dark, with a scar beneath his eye. The dark one smiled very contentedly. He nudged his associate, who did not smile, but whose eyes lighted coldly.

"Jessica Starbuck. And her manservant."

Jessie didn't respond. The Prussian looked at Santana and told him, "Your reward will be great, very great. I assure you of that."

The blond cartel man stepped forward and backhanded Ki. He spat out blood and stared back expressionlessly.

"Look, you—" Jessie began.

"My name," the dark-haired one said haughtily, "is Rundstedt."

"Not *von* Rundstedt? I thought all of you liked to affect those titles."

The Prussian sucked in air through his teeth. "It will give me great pleasure to see you die, Miss Starbuck."

"You're never going to see anything again if you don't get out of this cavern right now," Jessie replied. Even as they spoke, she had felt another earth movement underfoot.

"What do you mean?" Rundstedt demanded.

"What do you think I mean, you arrogant fool? Your blasting is knocking down this mesa. It's cut through with caverns and tunnels, it's weak and old and rotten. Your blasting is going to knock it to the ground."

"My engineer assures me that this is not the case."

"Then your engineer hasn't been up in the caves."

"You have?" Rundstedt's eyes brightened.

"Yes. We've been up through the mesa. All the way to the top. It's as rotten as . . . as the cartel."

Rundstedt was undisturbed by her remark. He frowned thoughtfully. "Why don't you want us to blast, Miss Starbuck? Let me guess."

"Guess away. Can we go outside, say about a half a mile away, while you guess?"

Rundstedt didn't respond to that at all. He looked at Ki and then back to Jessie. "You've seen it?" he asked.

"Yes."

"The galleon!" Rundstedt couldn't hold back his eagerness now. "You've actually seen it?"

"We have. And I think we're the last people who ever *will* see it—and live. Rundstedt, wake up. The place is falling down."

"You are so concerned for my safety," he said with an oily little smile.

172

"Concerned for these Indians you have working in here. They'll all die too."

"Did you hear, Karl?" he asked the blond man, who was totally impassive. "They have seen the galleon."

"I have heard. Kill the prisoners now?"

"No. Patience." Rundstedt began to pace. Behind him, they had cleared away the rubble and would soon be placing a fresh charge. A small bald man with glasses rushed around supervising things. The engineer, Jessie guessed. The man who was going to bring the mesa down and not only kill the Napai slaves and their masters but destroy two entire civilizations, that of the man-things, the Spaniards, and that of the ancient ones, marooned by time on top of this mesa in the middle of the desert.

"Listen, Rundstedt, it is no joke, no trick at all—you can't keep setting off dynamite charges down here."

"We shall do as we like. Our engineer has given us his assurances. Tell me, Miss Starbuck—" Rundstedt's eyes narrowed and grew cunning—"is it because we are too near that you wish us to stop? Are we perhaps so near that the next blast will see us through to the inner chamber where the golden galleon lies?"

Jessie looked to Ki for help, but he could only shake his head. There was no way they were going to talk Rundstedt out of doing exactly as he wished. The man would destroy them all.

"He isn't used to having the truth told to him, Jessie," Ki said. "In his world you lie to gain favor, lie so that you don't have to tell your superiors what they don't wish to hear, lie to shift blame, lie to make profit. He'll never believe us, not until the mesa begins to fall around his shoulders."

Santana, who wasn't used to so much talk, was growing edgy. Andojar—standing supported by two *bandidos*—

noticed that. "Another rat becomes nervous, Jessie."

"What the hell are you talking about?" Santana demanded. He jerked Andojar to him by his shirtfront.

Andojar laughed. "Nothing. Only let me tell you this. The mesa was full of rats, descendants of those aboard the galleon. They are gone now, Santana. Gone because they knew."

Santana was a superstitious man and a man of instinct. He didn't like that idea. The rats' departure seemed ominous to him.

"Ah, you lie, Andojar! You always lied."

Andojar looked the *bandido* leader straight in the eye. "As you like—but think back and recall the time when I lied to you, Santana. Recall a single time."

"Rats, rats!" Rundstedt said. "What is all this nonsense about rats?"

"He's ready," said the man called Karl. He pointed toward the engineer, who was running out some fuse from a charge of dynamite.

"Please," Jessie said, "let's go out into the open, call your laborers out. At least while this charge goes off."

"What is this?"

"The woman is afraid of noise, perhaps?" Karl and Rundstedt had themselves a chuckle over that. They were witty fellows; preparing to blow themselves and hundreds of other people up, they could still get off a joke.

Jessie clenched her teeth in anger and frustration. Ki was ready to slip his wrist bonds, but what good that would do, he didn't know. He could get to the fuse if it was lighted, yank it—and then be shot. That was about it. Fifteen seconds more life for those within and atop the mesa.

"Please . . ."

"Enough of this, woman!" Rundstedt said angrily, and slapped Jessie's face. Hard. Her head spun around and her

174

brain filled with cottony gray haze. She saw Andojar try to fight, only to be knocked down.

She shook her head but it wouldn't clear. There was a wild commotion of some kind to her left. Then her vision cleared and she saw the engineer waving everyone away, saw the fuse lighted. It sparked and hissed and wound across the cavern floor, and the engineer gave Rundstedt the thumbs-up sign.

"Madness," Jessie said, and Rundstedt only looked at her as, arms crossed, he watched the fuse burning short, and beyond the wall his dream glittered—his dream of wealth for the cartel, his dream of promotion, of honor, of reward.

Chapter 17

The fuse flickered and spat out tiny puffs of smoke. Somewhere inside the tunnel, a charge of dynamite waited to destroy the world.

The first shot came from Jessie's left, and she turned that way, ducking reflexively before she saw what had happened.

The Napai had come! And at their head was Gentle Night, with a captured rifle. The others had their ancient muskets— or hoes, or shovels, or rocks. They ran at the *bandidos*, war cries barely recalled, seldom used, rising from their throats as they struck back at Santana's men.

Ki slipped his wrist bonds, slammed the side of his hardened hand into the neck of the nearest guard, and leaped high, kicking Santana himself on the temple. The bandit chief's pistol discharged into the air as he fell backward.

Rundstedt tried to draw a pistol from a shoulder holster, but Jessie kicked it from his hand. Snatching it up, she leveled a telling shot at a *bandido* who was ready to kill a Napai laborer.

Ki was running through the turmoil toward the tunnel

where the fuse had turned the corner and was all too quickly making its way toward the charge beyond.

He ran in a crouch, leaping over rubble, racing the fuse and destruction. He threw himself the last fifteen feet and yanked the fuse from the charge. He sat there for a moment, breathing raggedly, then rolled to his feet, throwing the spent fuse aside, noting how little of it had been left.

He returned then to the cavern, where the savage fighting continued.

Santana's people had the firepower, but the Napai had righteous anger impelling them. They had been preyed upon too long. Some of them had been captured and used for slaves. Now the slaves had revolted, and they picked up whatever was at hand—picks, shovels, stones—and fought back.

Muskets bellowed and *bandidos* went down. Ki, fighting his way back toward Jessie, used three of his remaining *shuriken*, and there were three more dead *bandidos*.

Jessie still had the captured pistol, and she was two-handing it, fighting off Santana's people, who were slowly being pushed back, moving toward the back of the cavern.

Then she was clubbed down by an invisible hand. The earthquake struck again as she got to her hands and knees. Ki yanked her upright.

"We've got to leave. Now!" he said. Andojar, on his own feet, a gun in his left hand, started calling out to the Indians.

They didn't listen, not until Ki saw Gentle Night and managed to make her hear above the roar of guns, the cries of the dying.

"It's coming down now! We have to get out! Tell your people to back up!"

Gentle Night looked around her. The confusion was vast; there was fighting on every side. The Napai seemed to have gained the advantage. Even six-shooters have to click on empty chambers, and the Indians were unstoppable. Santana's people, hardened border raiders, backed up and even fled in panic into the heart of the mesa.

"No more!" Gentle Night shouted after them. "Now, let us retreat!"

They didn't hear her, or if they did, they weren't ready to back off. They wanted the blood of Santana's men. "Please! The mesa is falling!"

It was—unmistakably. Rock fell in huge sections from the ceiling. Walls of stone collapsed.

Andojar tried shouting at his people. "Come on! You are fighting for your lives. You will have no lives if you do not retreat."

A tremor, larger than any so far, got through to the common Napai mind more clearly than any shouted orders. People were knocked from their feet everywhere. A scaffolding fell.

Andojar started backing toward the cavern's entranceway himself, taking stock of things as he went. He saw Jessie with Ki, moving backward, still fighting. Gentle Night was alive. Rundstedt was dead. Andojar had shot him himself as the Prussian tried to crush his skull with a pickax. Karl had run to the back of the cave. Santana was nowhere to be seen, and that angered Andojar; he wanted that man, wanted him more than anything in his life. He wanted to put the *bandido* leader in his grave where he belonged, to bury him before he killed again and again.

"Andojar!" Ki shouted, and the former *bandido* turned, took to his heels, and raced toward the cavern mouth.

The Indians were rushing that way too now, fighting a running battle with Santana's men, who tried to surge forward from the recesses where they had taken shelter. Jessie slipped again, and as she got up she glanced toward the ceiling of the mesa. There was an awesome fissure forming there, gradually widening, like a devouring mouth. Stone dust was everywhere. People were screaming. There were cries of agony, or exultation, war cries. Mules brayed in panic.

Ahead of Jessie was the cavern mouth. Thirty feet, and then twenty, and the whole damn thing began to go.

The earth gods rumbled and howled and bellowed and groaned. Jessie saw the roof buckle and fall, saw people crushed beneath stone. A dozen of Santana's people went to their fate together as a vast section of cavern ceiling fell on them. Their eyes went wide, they threw up their puny arms to fend off the stone, but nothing would stop death, not even their futile curses or pathetic, feeble little prayers.

Outside, dust belched from the cavern mouth. Ki had Jessie's hand suddenly, and they were running across the desert floor, running as the mesa folded in on itself and collapsed with a sound like a dozen locomotives colliding, with a sound like the end of the world.

Jessie fell again and she just sat there, waving her hand helplessly, breathing in and out in deep gasps as the dust floated toward them in thick, roiling clouds.

After a time, Ki, who had been standing watching, sat beside her and they shared the silence. There was no mesa anymore, but only sad rubble, a crumbled monument to greed and futility, a tomb filled with lost ambitions and wishes, but there was no longer a mesa.

The river sprang up to the south, rising out of the ground like a liquid phoenix, and it flowed away southward, reborn. To the north, thunder rumbled again and it began to rain.

"Can we go home?" Gentle Night asked.

Jessie rose. She stood a moment longer, watching, the wind in her hair, the rain on her face. "Yes," she said. "Let's go home."

180

* * *

For Gentle Night, Vera Cruz was home. She had wanted
to go to the village of the Napai, but Andojar persuaded
her to stay at Vera Cruz and help with the mission. There
would be another priest from Spain, but that would take a
very long time. In the meantime, Andojar and Gentle Night
kept things running.

"All foolishness," Andojar said. "These people would
be better off in a city. Back on the reservation they have
nothing. And what's the good of waiting around here for
another priest to come? A waste of your life, kneeling in
church."

"You're here," Jessie said.

"Well—I do it for sentimental reasons," Andojar replied,
shrugging.

"Your father. The priest."

"My father. He was a *man*. I wish I had understood him
before." He looked into the distance briefly. The day was
bright, warm. Andojar wasn't very good at dissembling.

"Is Gentle Night still teaching the Indians English?"

"Yes, and she's good at it. For an Indian," Andojar added
hastily.

"And so what happens now, Andojar? After the new
priest comes, what happens to Andojar?"

"I don't know. What can I do? I have no skills except
those of the gun. I have nowhere to go. *Quién sabe?* Maybe
I will go south, across the border."

"As an outlaw?"

"Again, *quién sabe?* Who knows? I have been told there
are fights to the south worth the fighting. Good fights where
people are trying to keep slave masters from taking them
from their families and putting them in chains."

"Is that the life for you?"

"Perhaps." He was thoughtful. "I must fight. I know I

181

must. I know too that one day, if I do not leave, someone will gather the courage to come and kill me. There is money on my head still, Jessie. They will come, and if I have grown fat and placid, they will kill me."

"And so you ride?"

He looked to the mission. "Soon. Yes, soon I ride." He put his arm suddenly around Jessie and kissed her deeply until her blood began to course through her body. "Would you go with me one more time onto the desert? Once more before you leave me?"

"One more time," she said. She kissed him again and then waited—impatiently—while he went to saddle two horses.

They rode southward, speaking little. The great mound of rubble which had been Mesa Grande was before them. It was a sobering sight.

"But you see," Andojar said, "life goes on." Before them was the village of the Napai, where people planted corn and rebuilt their lodges, where children and dogs played in the dust.

"I don't want to go to the mesa," Jessie objected.

"Come," Andojar coaxed. "I want to show you something."

"All right."

They rode toward it and up the narrow canyon, which still existed. Andojar swung down from his horse and beckoned to Jessie. She swung down as well and they walked up the canyon, leading their horses.

"Up here," Andojar said, turning up the feeder canyon. "You see?"

The stone pictures were still there, carved into the canyon walls: the great galleon, the coming of the Spaniards, the pictograph of the mesa.

"It exists still. The very ancient." He looked back again toward the village of the Napai. "And the new. They continue. We continue. Come with me, Jessie Starbuck, and lie down with me upon the ground."

She followed him to the pool, which was still there as well, placid now and peaceful. She stepped from her clothes, as did Andojar, and went into his arms to feel the close press of his sun-warmed naked body, to feel his chest flatten her breasts pleasantly, to feel the strength of his erection nuzzling her abdomen.

They were interrupted. "Sorry, Andojar," the voice said, "you're not getting it."

Santana stood there, a gun in his hand. His shirt was ripped, his face whiskered. His nose was misshapen. His right boot was split open.

"What do you want?" Andojar demanded.

"What do you think? You. Dead. You still owe me. You and the woman here. You took away everything I had; I have nothing, no one. You destroyed it all. First you turned your back to me and then you came back and destroyed it all!"

There was the light of madness in his eye. He shook, his head moving uncertainly on his neck. His leg twitched. Only the gun hand was rock-steady. Jessie could see the hammer on that big blue Colt drawn back, could see the deadly intent in Santana's eyes. Andojar's guns were ten feet away, lying with his clothes. Jessie's was not quite so far. Six feet. And Santana's attention was on Andojar.

She edged that way, and the muzzle of Santana's gun suddenly moved toward her.

"Stand still, girl!" he commanded. Jessie stopped. Andojar shook his head slightly, imploring her not to try it, but what other choice was there?

The pool was quiet and deep blue beneath the palms. A crow circled overhead. The breeze was gentle through the trees.

"It's time, Andojar," Santana said. "Time to die."

He lifted the pistol to arm's length, and Jessie dove for her gun. She yanked it from its holster and rolled, coming up firing as Santana shot past her, chipping stone from a great gray boulder.

Jessie brought up the .38 and fired three times. Santana was jerked backward, his hands waving feebly. His eyes were filled with pain, his mouth with blood. He toppled into the desert pond and lay there, floating.

Jessie lowered the pistol and Andojar came to her and held her tightly against him.

"Thank you, Jessie. Damn it, it's a wonder he didn't kill you. It was the last thing I wanted you to try, but thank God you did."

"There wasn't much choice," she said. "You made me some promises, and he wanted to keep you from fulfilling them. I couldn't let him do that."

"No, I guess not," Andojar said, and they clung to each other, naked, warmed by the blessed heat and light of the sun, the last memory of darkness and death and terror now behind them, and ahead of them only their deep need for each other . . .

Watch for

LONE STAR AND THE RIO GRANDE BANDITS

thirty-fourth novel in the exciting
LONE STAR
series from Jove

coming in June!